UNDERLYING GRACE

A JOURNEY TO FIND MORE IN LIFE

G. ALLEN MERCER

UNDERLYING GRACE

A JOURNEY TO FIND MORE IN LIFE

G. ALLEN MERCER

TABLE OF CONTENTS

Underlying Grace

Copyright © 2014 by G. Allen Mercer

For Christine, Justin and Audrey

PROLOGUE

I feel conflicted, ashamed, and out of control. It seems that everything I do in order to save my family puts me one step closer to our demise.

Prayer works, at least I think it does. So, in the pinnacle of the worst crisis in my life, why do I feel such a disconnect from God? Where has He been all of my life? Why do I feel like we are suffering needlessly? Why do I feel like I am on the wrong path in life? Why do I think that no one else can grasp the problems that I am facing? I ask myself. No, I ask God: Are you listening?

< >

We found this great radio station earlier in the day, but it only came through when the road flowed out into the valleys. But now, at night, high in the mountains, the road was curvy and narrow, the fog was thick, and the radio station was mostly static. The tension in the car was almost as thick as the fog. We had been arguing about small stuff—money mostly—for the last hour. It was our anniversary, and we were tired and irritable after driving for most of the day. So, regardless of how bad the fog was outside, or how bad the static was on the radio, or how much we bit each other's heads off, we knew that there was a mountain condo waiting for us just a few more miles up the road. This was our goal. This is what we needed. At least, we thought it was.

Claire leaned forward to adjust the radio again. Neil could see that she was trying to think of something that would break the tension and help them focus on the weekend. Turning the radio off and clearing the noise might be the best thing she could have done, but she asked a question instead.

"Do you think the kids are okay?"

That was the last thing I heard my wife say before we hit the 18-wheeler head on.

CHAPTER 1

"I thought it was foggy."

"It is down there."

"Then why can we see so clearly?"

"My, you do have a lot of questions. I have always admired that trait in you."

"But if it was foggy, why can we see them so clearly?

"I can make it foggy here as well, if you want."

"I…I…don't know what I want."

"Yes, I know. That is one of the reasons why we are talking."

The scene below was one of carnage. The night fog was cut by the rhythmic blink of emergency lights and flares that marked a slow path around the crash site. The white Suburban, with all of its steel and stability, was no match for the tractor trailer. It was not clear who was at fault, but it was clear that someone had died.

"Perhaps we should take a walk, you know, to clear your head. I know this great path. Walk it with me."

"No." Neil resisted. "I want to see what happens. Are they going…you know…to be alright, to make it?"

"I feel that they will be alright, so, why don't we take that walk now." The other man waved his arm for Neil to follow.

Neil turned away from the scene, the fog drifting away from his body, but still stagnated in his mind. He put one foot out and started walking toward the man.

"Who are you exactly?" Neil gazed at the denim covered back of the older man, for the first time really acknowledging his presence. The blue in his jacket was slightly faded and the jacket looked comforting, like an old friend.

The older man, Neil would call him a gentleman, turned around slowly, revealing round tin-colored glasses, cool blue eyes, and salt-and-pepper hair, heavy on the salt. His face was warm and wrinkled slightly. The creases across his forehead curved as he raised an eyebrow at the young man.

"Well?"

"Well what?" Neil responded.

"Am I what you expected?"

"What do you mean?"

"Do I cut the mustard, pass with flying colors, am I all that I'm cracked up to be?" The older gentleman pushed his lips together, not letting the younger man answer. "Follow me. We have a long path ahead of us."

Without any further words, Neil fell in line behind the older man, who's faded cargo pants jingled with something in one of the side pockets every other step or two.

After what seemed to be thirty minutes or so of walking, Neil felt a pinch in his side. He was having a hard time keeping up with the older man. Grabbing the cramp in his side with one hand, he turned the other over and wiped his left forearm across his brow, leaving a stream of glisten that flattened the hairs on his arm.

"You know…"

"Yes?" the Old Man said, before Neil could finish.

Neil shot the back of the man a stern look and bounded a step or two ahead, stopping the Old Man in his tracks. The Old Man had been watching the stones in the path ahead of them and was not shocked at the younger man's launch forward, but, regardless, he seemed to smile at the change in character.

"You know," Neil started again, for the first time looking the man in the eyes. His eyes were not just blue, but, behind the glass of the tin-rimmed glasses, he could see that they were more lightly grey with streaks of blue, like the side of a glacier before it tumbles into the ocean.

"You keep saying that, and then you stop," the Old Man said, meeting Neil's stare and looking deep into his soul.

Neil could feel it. It was as if being scanned by the most powerful X-ray machine on the planet. He felt naked, as if he were standing in the middle of a football field during the championship game and it was being covered by every television station in the world. Besides the feeling of soul-stripping exposure, Neil also felt mercy, love, and the tendrils of grace. The feelings warmed him and covered his exposure like a pile of soft fluffy towels fresh out of the dryer. He didn't want the feeling to go away, but as reality snapped back to his body, he found himself still looking at those blue eyes.

"What?" Neil eeked out, his throat was dry as a bone. He tried swallowing. He tried looking away from the man. He could do neither.

The older man let his eyes drink in the emotions of the younger man's face. He smiled, bringing the younger man back to full focus. He was slow to speak and let Neil absorb each of his words.

"You keep saying, 'You know,' and then you stop. Actually, most times I do know, but it is more beneficial if you tell me. Most say I am a good listener. Some even say I am a good speaker. I like to think I am a little of both, with a passion to tell a good story." And with that, the older man stepped past Neil and continued up the rocky path, the gravity of grace pulling Neil after him.

Neil could feel the tug of something coarse and abrasive versus something warm and good wrestle in his soul. He took a step toward the older man…warm and good…and then stopped. Doubt fought its way into his thoughts and forced him to look back down the trail, back from where they had just come. With sudden clarity, he could still see the accident, even through they had been walking for a long time. He took a step toward it and froze, his body began to tremble, and the warm sweat that he had once wiped from his brow now seemed cold and clammy. He tried to swallow, but it was if he had a lump in his throat preventing anything from passing. He took another tentative step toward the wreck. What was distant and manageable was now on top of him and chaotic; doubt filled his mind…*What happened to the people*?

"Neil," a voice said from just behind him, breaking through the clouds of doubt that had so easily swirled to paralyze him. "Are you coming?"

Neil did not answer. He felt as though his feet had been cemented to the ground, his arms felt bound to his sides, and his hands clenched, his knuckles white from anger and stress.

"Neil," the man said again, this time placing a hand on his shoulder.

Neil turned slowly, unable to face the man again. He was ashamed that he had so easily let go of the gift that he had just received, the grace that had warmed his soul. He looked the man in the eyes with humble sorrow.

"Son, are you coming with me?"

Neil locked onto the man's eyes for support and took a step toward him. "I am here, I am with you," he said, accepting whatever path he was about to be led on.

CHAPTER 2

Neil watched her from behind as she gently moved her foot, touching the wood deck every so often in order to keep the hammock dancing in the rhythm of the setting sun. She was beautiful, and they were both young. He watched her wavy blond hair poke through the ropes, no doubt causing patterns that she would later regret. He could feel something, an emotion that was tantalizing and warm. Although he wasn't quite sure what it was, he wanted to feel more of it.

"Can I sit with you?" Neil asked, sliding up beside her.

"Sure," she said, slowing the hammock long enough for him to slide in next to her.

"It is a good party."

"Thanks, I hope my parents don't find out." She glanced through the screen door at the party going on inside; no one had broken anything…yet.

"It's your birthday for crying out loud, that's what they get for being out of town. Besides, I think everyone is cool in there. They all respect you and your parents. They might even help clean up," the young Neil said with a witty grin.

"Sure, I guess so," Claire said, smiling at the small attempt at humor, and then looking away from the boy that she was falling for. He was so young; a full two grades younger than she was, and she was about to go to college. *Should I even get into a relationship now?* But this was not the time to think about what should not happen; this was a time to think about what could happen. With one more glance over her shoulder to see who was around, she slid her hand into his as she pushed off on the hammock again.

When you are young, there is nothing but time, and Neil knew that what he was doing, just swinging back and forth with this beautiful girl, was the only thing he wanted to do, and he knew that he wanted to do it for a long time.

He was the first to see a shooting star, and before he could beg her to make a wish, Claire saw the second, and then before either of them knew, their lips touched, followed by a deep kiss. With a mutual wish granted, and fulfilled, they both sat back in the hammock and rocked; Neil was sure that he was seeing more than shooting stars...fireworks, he was sure they were fireworks.

For more than an hour, the two held hands on the back deck of her parent's house while well-wishing friends stayed inside with the bottle of gin someone had stolen from their parent's liquor cabinet. They thought it best to give the two lovebirds space; everyone could see they were crazy for each other.

<>

"What were you thinking about?" the Old Man asked. They had continued their walk up the mountain trail; Neil had stopped shaking. He had, for the most part, stopped doubting and was just kind of going with the flow of being there…walking. He really didn't have an answer. He was just walking; walking…and letting old memories wash back into his soul.

"Hold onto those feelings, son," the Old Man said, turning to look at him. "True, raw love is genuine and special. It can transcend time and help you in the darkest times…and often, it is those experiences, the ones of pure love, that anchor you the most," the Old Man finished, without being prodded to expound or knowing what Neil had been thinking about.

Neil watched the Old Man speak, but he really didn't hear what he was saying. He was trying to grasp at the edges of the memory of his young escapade with Claire as it slowly faded in his head. He closed his eyes for a second and rubbed his head with the palm of his hands to slowly bring himself back to where he was. He opened his eyes still not knowing. He was confused. The memory and the feeling were gone. He had let the feelings, thoughts, and love slip just beyond his grasp. He shivered.

"Where are we walking to?"

"Well, up here a bit," the Old Man said with simplicity. "Remember, I told you it would take a while."

"A while to what?" Neil was quick to agitate. Anger warmed him and stopped the shivering. "Where are we walking to?" he demanded, his nerves raw with the pain of the wreck, the lost memories…the lost love. "I don't even know where the hell I am!"

The Old Man studied the younger man as he thrashed the memories and feelings around in his soul. This was something that the Old Man knew must happen, much like a drunk coming off of a lifetime of binge drinking. It was hard to watch, but the end result was worth the journey. He had led many people down similar paths, and they all seemed to follow a familiar course—start with what grounds you and build off of that.

Neil paid no attention to the Old Man staring at him. He was consumed with his memories…memories stronger and more vivid than he had ever experienced before! But even with their clarity, he had no control over them. They just came and went, as if guided by someone else. Neil rubbed his head again; the feelings of love were crashing at the edge of his soul, trying to break down whatever walls were there to protect him.

"Where is Claire?" he yelled, unsure where the outburst had come from.

"Son, if you look deeper into your feelings you will find the answers to the torment that is burning in your soul. It is dark in there, I know, but if you let me, we can work through the barriers and you can rise from the ashes of a broken life," the Old Man said, putting both of his hands on Neil's shoulders.

Neil absorbed the touch of the hands as strength. He checked his anger and doubt again, trying to push them into a place somewhere deep inside. He knew it would be a task to keep these emotions locked in that dark place long...but he would try.

The Old Man released Neil's shoulders and walked a few feet up the path. He was smiling to himself, knowing that it was precisely those two emotions—anger and doubt—that he wanted to pull out of the man.

"Come here," the Old Man motioned Neil up alongside of him. He paid no attention to the indecision of youth.

Neil trudged obediently up the path, coming shoulder to shoulder with his guide. They were standing at the top of a ridge. The wind blew, but not in a way in which to knock them down, but in a way in which to envelope them and cradle them safely.

"What?" Neil asked, straightening up his back and looking in the direction in which the Old Man was pointing.

"There are stages in a man's life when he needs to reflect on the times that he has had, the times he has, and the times that he will have. This place…this place in which we are about to enter is just such a place in which to seek these times. In this place you can find out things about yourself that you have forgotten and things that you did not know existed. This is the place where the light meets the dark and where the healing begins," the Old Man said, sweeping his arm across the sky just as thousands of shooting stars seemed to follow his fingertips.

Neil watched for a moment, his mind now far away from the people in the accident. He had no idea what the Old Man was saying, and for that matter, he really didn't care…yet.

The Old Man sensed what the younger man felt; something that he had sensed millions of times in the souls of the millions that had come before Neil.

"You have questions and you will have a decision to make based on the answers to those questions. I can help you find the answers, but it is you that must make the decisions. In order to do this, to make these decisions, you must find the well of your passion and draw from its depths…you must believe in yourself, and you must…" the Old Man clenched his fist and gently put it to his lips before whispering the following. "And…you must believe…believe in me."

Neil's eyes refocused away from the stars, and he turned his head to look at the Old Man, his mind suddenly fluttered with questions. *Who was this person? Why must I believe in him? What decision must I make? What is my passion? What answers did he have? Where am I? Where is my wife? Where are my children? Are they safe? Why must I believe in this old man?*

"See, I told you that you had many questions," the Old Man said, reaching up to grip Neil on the shoulder. "Now, let's explore this path together…I will always be with you, and I can promise that we will find some answers; but first, let us explore. Come!"

Neil watched as the man started down the other side of the mountain, the mist of the mountain rising up to meet him, swallow him up, and cover his tracks with a mystical calm. The mountaintop seemed a little darker once the man disappeared.

"How does this man know so much about me," Neil whispered to himself, suddenly too scared to move. He felt alone, now that the fog had swallowed the man. To Neil, this was the same fog that always clouded his mind, the same fog that shrouded him from seeing the wreck clearly, the same fog that filled him with anger, the same fog that was always in his mind when he tried to talk to God, the same fog that…

"Neil," a voice said, cutting through the torture in his mind. "You may be standing on the path, but it is only a path if you walk along it," the Old Man said, reappearing to retrieve the lost soul; and with a smile, he turned his back in a motion to follow.

Neil, feeling not so alone, took a step down the path to follow him.

CHAPTER 3

The check represented the largest sum of money he had ever held in his hands. Which were now trembling.

"Are you alright Mr. Abrams?" the teller asked, sensing the excitement on her customer's face.

"Yes, of course! This is the best day ever," he said, and then proudly exclaimed to the bank teller, and everyone in the line, that this check was to be the down payment on their first house. The smile of approval from people he would never know was something that he would carry with him for years and years.

A shade over $7,000 represented a year's worth of savings. It represented a year's worth of not eating out, a year's worth of not having wine, buying each other gifts, vacations, or anything. But today, this check, this tiny piece of paper represented the next step of adulthood; the next step in their life—their first house.

After looking at dozens and dozens of starter homes, homes that needed work, and homes that they could never afford, they finally found one that was all about them: A three-bedroom split-level with a real fireplace on an acre of land dotted by 30-year-old pine trees and the most beautifully ugly apple tree. This was theirs. This would be the place where their firstborn would be conceived and the place where they would start to build memories. This would be the place that would always represent the simple life; the life before carpool, quarterly taxes, and major responsibilities. This simple house would be the place before career decisions, college tuition, wedding planning, and horse camp. This would be the place where they would come very close to being killed.

"I can't get it any closer!" Neil yelled out of the cracked window of the moving truck. The rain was beating down on the couple just twenty-four hours after the loan closing. Moving day had been anything but a breeze. The elevator at the apartment was broken and moving from their third-floor flat had taken longer than they had planned. It didn't help that all of their friends had "conveniently" found other things to do…and now the rain was coming down in buckets! But, rain or no rain, they loved each other, and this was going to be their first night in their new home, come hell or high water.

"That's good there," Claire said, holding one hand up to the vision of her husband in the side mirror and slapping the truck with the other. "We'll just have to deal with the rain. Come help me extend the ramp," she yelled from the shelter of the open garage. She too was ready to start the life they had both dreamed of. Claire watched her husband exit the driver's side of the moving truck and duck his head in a veiled attempt to block the rain. As he ran back to the garage, she stepped in front of him at the point where the rain fell freely from the roof with the most intensity.

"What are—"

She put her hands on his face as the water beat off his head and kissed him like never before.

"Wow! I guess it only gets better from here, huh?"

"I love you," she said smiling, and wiped the water across his face before turning back to the truck. "If we had to get wet, might as well make it good!"

Neil nodded at the logic and lifted the gate to reveal their life's possessions.

"Do you think I can try with the beer and the pizza again?" Neil asked, in another veiled attempt to persuade his wife that their friends could be convinced to come to the rescue.

"I think it's just us from here on out dear," she said pulling the ramp down.

Neil looked up at the sky. "Yea, I think you're right."

The pair moved to tackle the job. It was just the two of them; something that they would build on and always count on. For without the other, there was not one. They were a team, partners, spouses, and soul mates. Although each could manage without the other, they had realized that they worked best together; something that would carry them through the rest of their lives together…they were always stronger together.

Except for the kiss, the day seemed exceedingly uneventful. The boxes stacked up in the kitchen and in their bedroom, but in reality, there really wasn't that much stuff. The work passed with thoughts about fixing this or changing that. Before the truck was unloaded, Neal had mapped out the new kitchen he was going to build, and Claire had decided to build bluebird boxes and put them along the back fence.

"I am going to put all of the plants on the front porch," Neil said, halfway through the move. "Maybe they'll get some water, seeing that the gutters are overflowing! Guess I've got my first item on the honey-do list," Neil jokingly yelled through the screen door.

"Oh, that list is growing by the hour hun!"

< >

"Do you remember what happened next?" the Old Man asked, without looking at Neil. They were sitting on two boulders watching the first wisps of the pink sunrise flow over the mountains and warm their day.

Neil was lost in the beauty of the memory; it was washing through his mind like a pleasant float down a tranquil river, with no knowledge of the danger around the next bend.

"Yea." His voice was flat and his eyes unfocused, as if seated on the back row of the theater. "I took the plants onto the front porch, and it was raining to beat the band. I just kept looking up at the gutters and the pine trees and thinking that I was always going to be getting pine needles out the gutters forever…"

"And?"

"And that's when I saw it."

"What did you see?"

"I saw evil."

The Old Man let the presence burn the man's being for a second before nudging him from the thought. "Yes, go on."

"It was the most evil-looking opening in the sky. Black. Livid. Hungry. Like an angry giant corkscrew, it popped over the ridge about four houses down from us. I saw colossal oaks being lifted out of the ground like they were part of a child's miniature railroad play set. It was terrifying."

"Yes it was, and do you recall what you did?"

"Yea, I knew…I knew right then…I heard it…the train sound, and the oaks snapping, the wind was pushing and pulling all at once. One of our ferns flew off the railing and never returned. I…I knew what it was. All I could think of was Claire."

"What did you do?" The Old Man asked again, his voice calm.

"I dropped the other plant and ran inside."

< >

"Get in the damn basement! *Now!*"

"*What is it?*" Claire yelled, seeing the horror on his face. But she already knew. She could see the blackness of evil and hear the roar of Hell at their new doorstep.

The front yard started transforming before her eyes. She saw a vortex spinning toward them, like an angry black bulldozer chewing up everything in its path. The front screen door came off its hinges snapping her back into reality. She looked at Neil, who was screaming at her.

"*Claire! Claire!*" he screamed, spinning her by the shoulders and pulling her from her trance. "*It's a tornado!*"

< >

"You reacted."

"I reacted…I grabbed her arm, we scooped up the cat, and ran for the garage."

"Tell me what you felt?"

< >

"Neil, Oh God!" Claire was screaming as they hunched down at the bottom of the stairs. Although there was panic in her voice, she was not crying. This was not a time to cry with tears; this was a time to cry out in desperate prayer. The house was trembling, at the verge of implosion. Neil could hear the straining of the structure as it fought to hold onto its foundation and as it fought to keep its new owners safe.

"It will be okay. We will be okay," he answered her screams. He tried to look up, but his wife's grip held his head down to protect him. She had put her head between the impending evil and his. He wrapped his arms around her to hold her to him. He hooked his leg through the 2x6 stair as a last-ditch measure. He would never let her go…no matter what.

< >

Neil searched his heart and then his memory, trying to recall the exact sensation. "I felt fear, primal fear; the kind of fear that grips you at night after a nightmare…when you are sure there is evil in the bedroom, but you don't want to open your eyes and look." Neil wiped the sweat off his forehead again. "But, then…"

"Yes, and then what? What did you feel son?" The Old Man seemed excited about the outcome.

"I don't know? She was holding my head down so tight and screaming. The trees outside were exploding, falling and hitting the ground with thunderclaps like cannons. The pressure was so intense; like a vice was squeezing my head…the vibrations rang through my chest. But…but, I felt a sense of calm, almost like we had arms around us. The house seemed to be exploding, but we were safe; insulated by…by…"

"By what son?"

"I don't know…I can't describe it. Maybe it was God, or maybe it was something else."

The Old Man thought about this for a moment, taking in a deep breath and letting it out slowly. Neither man spoke for a while, both lost in thought and emotion. The sunrise climbed above the mountains, erasing the darkness and brightening the world.

"We," Neil said, clearing his throat to find his voice. "We were okay. We…the house…everything was okay." He looked at the Old Man, searching his face for a reaction. He saw compassion and understanding. "You…it was…," his voice trailed off to a whisper, and he couldn't say the rest of the sentence.

The Old Man smiled. "It will be alright son." He let the moments of silence nurse the younger man's wounds, which allowed him to rediscover his voice.

"The house, us, even the cat…we were all okay. The yard was a mess, we lost nearly every tree on the lot, but the tornado…it…it just, and I still don't know how, but it just missed us. Afterward, when we walked the path of the storm, every other house on the street was hit, except ours. I don't know how it did it…I guess we were just blessed that day."

The Old Man stood up from the boulder, brushed off his pants, and covered his eyes to take in the beauty of the rising sun.

"Son, I think it is time that you realized that you are blessed every day; but it shouldn't take the clear evidence of a miracle to prove it to you." And with that, he started down the path again, leaving Neil to ponder the glory of what was in front of him.

CHAPTER 4

For the next hour, they walked along the edges of fields, where Neil saw several rabbits dart in and out of their path. Wisps of mountain fog rolled along the top of the tree lines like translucent cloud spirits. Their final dance of the new morning ebbed and flowed with the light breezes among the valleys as they slowly dissolved in the sunbeams of the day. Occasionally there was a rustle of a dry leaf from a squirrel rummaging for food or the calling of one tree frog to another, but what Neil seemed to hear the most was the babble of a distant stream. This was a sound that, in his youth, was always one of exploration and adventure. The sound made him smile, and like sounds or smells can do, it brought back fond memories.

"Your mood has changed," the older man said across his shoulder. He was still leading the way along the path.

Neil stopped cold in his tracks, as did the Old Man three paces in front of him. Realization filled his mind and warmed his body.

"Did it really take you that long to figure this out," the Old Man asked without turning around? He smiled to himself. He always loved this exact moment: The moment when someone figured *it* out. He had seen Neil "figure this out" a few other times in his life, only to lose the connection; but this time…this was the one that was really going to count.

"No," Neil said quietly, "I kind of thought it through when we were talking about the tornado, but…" He hesitated. "I kind of just thought it might be different."

"What did you think would be so different," the Old Man said briskly, finally turning and focusing the ice-blue eyes again into Neil's soul. "Certainly you did not think that I would be different? This is how you have always seen me."

"How I have always seen you…but…I have never seen you."

"Really son, do you want me to go there?" the Old Man said with a sly grin.

Neil raised an eyebrow as if to say, "Yea, I do."

"Fine," the Old Man said, shaking his head. "When you were lost in the field, one very similar to this one," he said waving at the one they were standing next to. "Don't think too hard. You were five. Yes, you were five, and your stepfather had tossed a ball out into the field to let you find it. They were taking pictures of the sun as it set. You felt alone, as you often did growing up, and at that point, the ball was all you had. Do you remember?"

Neil scrunched his forehead together, letting the memory flood his thoughts. The smell of the creek mud as it squished in his red Converse shoes washed over his senses. The yellow light of the setting sun cast its dark shadows along the paths. Each shadow seemed to block his way. And then there were the reeds, as tall as he hoped to be when he reached six…if he ever reached six. His stepfather had recently told him the three little pigs story, and this was the type of field that the wolf would live in, he was sure of it.

"Do you remember the—"

"Turtle, yea," Neil said cutting him off. "I found it along one of the creek beds that I was following. It was sitting next to the ball. I remember wanting to take it back and show my stepfather, but I didn't, and I let it walk off into the reeds."

"What did you do then?"

"I…I grabbed the ball, and started after the turtle, but I couldn't find it again, the next thing I knew, I was back at the car." Neil rubbed his forehead, something he did when tired, or struck by a realization. "It was…it was you? You sent the turtle."

The Old Man looked him over with a raised eyebrow as if to answer Neil's early gesture, with a "see, I told you so."

"But it was just a silly turtle." Neil tossed the doubt in his mind.

"Perhaps," the Old Man responded to Neil's thoughts. "But to you, at that moment in time, it was a friend, a guide, and something that helped you. Silly? Perhaps, but to a five-year-old, it was the perfect thing at the right time."

Neil refocused on the man. Questions beyond the significance of the turtle swirled in his head as he tried to process what this was all about. A thought, a dark thought, crept into his mind.

"Yes, son? Go ahead and get it out."

"If I am dead, I don't want this to be it, I mean not like this! I…I want Claire with me," Neil said, his voice cracking slightly. "I know that is selfish…I just love her so much. I…I didn't mean it!"

"Yes you did, otherwise you would not have said it with passion. I like the passion. It is what I am all about."

"But…"

The old man held his hand up to stop him from speaking. "Neil, who said you're dead?" And with that, the Old Man bent over and picked up a hefty-size stick that had fallen across the path. With a heave, the Old Man threw it into the fog that hovered above the creek. A second later, there was a splash.

Neil wiped a tear from his eye and looked in the direction of the splash. "Why did you do that?"

"That stick has been on this path for quite some time, yet I just moved it and made an impact on the stick and the river. The stick will start a new life, perhaps it will slowly float down the stream, or perhaps it will lodge itself along a large bolder, catch another floating twig, which would be the makings of a dam and ultimately a great lake. The point is that you, like the stick, are being moved onto another path. It will be your choice to float down the stream or build a lake."

Neil studied the wrinkles around the man's eyes. They made his face strangely comfortable, warm.

"I wish I knew what in the world you were talking about," Neil said, shaking his head. "I asked if I am dead and about Claire, and you throw sticks into the fog and talk about making lakes. Who are you, Yoda, or something?"

The Old Man smiled and acknowledged that he still had work to do in order to break through the younger man's defenses. "Let's keep walking along the stream. There are some more things I would like you to see."

Neil hesitated, he had not received any answers, and his worry for Claire burned inside him like a furnace.

"Son, Claire is fine, she is in good hands," the Old Man said, putting his hand on Neil's shoulder and nudging him toward the sound of water. Neil slowly put one foot in front of the other, and briefly thought he spotted a turtle disappearing off the path in front of them.

CHAPTER 5

The pair walked along next to the stream. Every so often, the stream would feed into a larger stream, and finally, a few more streams added their volume. As they walked, the body of moving water grew with every new step. The pebbles of the earlier stream had grown into boulders that stood against the strength of the flowing water; they channeled the water to their will. For a while, the only sound they heard was the noise of the water fighting the stones, but with every new step, the sounds of the water skirmish slowly grew to the roar of a water war.

Neil thought he knew what the sound was, and it sounded close, but his greater concern was staying on the path. As the volume of the crashing water had increased, so had the angle of the slope along the river. He was now leaning to his left side, having to use his hand as a stabilizer every once in awhile. It wasn't really a dangerous path, but one that needed intense concentration and sure foot placement. Neil wanted to talk, something he had not really been interested in doing before. He found that the hike and his sideways position behind the Old Man made it difficult to breach a conversation; and that is when the Old Man decided to speak.

"Earlier, we spoke about passion," the Old Man said, without turning around.

Neil just looked at the back of the man; he was also at an angle, but having a much better time with it. "Passion, right." He put his right foot between two deep roots and stepped over the hazard.

"Passion is the fuel of love," the Old Man said simply.

"Okay… so… what's that suppose to mean anyway?"

"Your love for Claire for instance."

"Okay, what about it? We have…had passion," Neil said, suddenly thinking about all of the arguments, the loss of his company, everything. It suddenly hit him hard. *I've cut her out...he's right! We don't have the passion anymore.*

"Neil, somewhere between where you were and where you are today, you lost sight of what it takes to fuel the gift of love. Son, you must work at love, you must work at passion. Sure, they can just happen, but to create something that you can sustain, you must tap into something that you can draw fuel from."

Neil suddenly looked worried. *Have I really let it die? How do I get it back? I do love her...*

"Yes, I know, you have told me quite loudly many times...perhaps it is time to remember something that can anchor you, something to draw off of, something to always come back to, something to fuel the passion. Here, take a look at this," the older man said, pushing aside some low hanging spruce branches and revealing a ledge. "If this does not inspire passion, I don't know what will."

Neil stepped past the branches and a rush of cool moist air rolled over him, carrying the strong scent of spruce. But, it was the roar of the falling water that filled his senses with cascading waves of power.

"Step through," the man said pushing the opening a little larger.

Neil stepped through, allowing the powerful scene to tap into something deeper inside...a well of passion that he had forgotten about.

< >

"Where are we going?"

"I can't tell you. Just grab the picnic stuff so we can get going!"

"Go where? There's nothing here but woods, and an old church."

They had been driving for nearly three hours...thirty minutes of that in four-wheel drive, as Neil's blue Jeep navigated the old Appalachian logging road. They had enjoyed the ride up from Atlanta, stopping at some antique shops along the way. Neil had accidently pronounced it "anti-Q,"starting a word that would always be theirs. They had laughed so hard that other people looked at them with sideways glances and whispered comments. It didn't matter to the happy young couple. They were just happy that they were not yet anti-Qs!

Neil navigated the Jeep to the grassy lot behind a small primitive Baptist church from the 1800s. He set the parking brake and breathed in the deep cool shade of the mountain oaks.

"Wow, God is even out here!" Claire said, looking over her shoulder at the faded white structure. She jumped out of the Jeep and ran up to the church.

"He is, and I can't wait to show you what He has done for us." Neil yelled over his shoulder. He watched her from his side mirror as she pressed her hands and face against the old lead glass of the church trying to spy God's primitive dwelling. "Come on, we need to follow this trail."

Neil had planned this day for months. The first time he had come here with his college dorm friends, he knew this would be the place…one day.

"It's is just a little farther."

Claire smiled at the back of her boyfriend's head. He was up to something, and she kind of had an idea, but that was crazy. He was still so young. She smiled; because that was the same thing she had thought all those years earlier on her parent's hammock.

"It's right up here!"

She could smell it before they were there, and the roar called to her through the leaves like a shepherd calls his flock.

"Take a look at that," Neil said, taking her hand and leading her down to the ledge of the falls.

"It's beautiful!"

"Yea, can you believe I have rappelled this…twice!"

"You're nuts," she said giddy with passion for the place and for her boyfriend.

"Perhaps," Neil said, looking around. "Let's have lunch…there," he pointed to a smooth rock a few pools up from the falls, which would allow them to spread a blanket out and still see the view.

Claire spread the blanket, being sure to check the edges of the pools for critters or snakes. She was still a little unsure of what Neil was up to. She watched him spread out the food and plates and open the wine. She leaned over and kissed him gently as he twisted the cork. He stopped long enough to accept the kiss and then poured them both a drink of the white wine into fake plastic wine cups.

"A toast!"

"What are we toasting?"

"Oh, I can think of some things," Neil said shyly.

"Yea, like what?"

"How about to the day. It's so beautiful, like it was made for us."

"Okay, what else?"

"To the sound of these falls."

"And?"

Neil stood up, holding his glass to the expanse over the falls. "*To my love! To you Claire!*" he yelled out to the openness.

She giggled and went to take a sip of her wine.

"Wait! There's more!"

"Oh I can't wait to hear this," she said, pulling the glass from her lips.

He bent down on one knee, looking her in the eyes. "All that I have to give you is love. One day I may be able to give you any material thing in the world, but I will still only want to give you the one true thing that I will ever possess—my love." Neil set his drink down and took her hand. "If you will let me, I would like to give you a lifetime of that love. Claire, will you marry me?"

He pulled a ring box out of his pocket and opened the box.

Claire looked at the ring, and this whacky man that she felt so much for and could barely get the word out. "Yes!"

Neil kissed her deeply, put the ring on her finger, and then jumped up to the edge of the falls. "*She said yes*! *Did you hear that? She loves me! She said yes!*"

<>

"Of course I heard you son. Now do you think you have enough fuel for the fire?"

CHAPTER 6

Claire's pregnancy had not been a simple one. It had taken them nearly a year to finally get pregnant. "Not for lack of trying!" Neil would often say to her, with a sly grin that she always met with her own knowing smile. The fun part of making a baby had evolved into duty, but they always pressed on. Having a baby had taken on a life of its own.

The pressure to become pregnant was intense. Their best friends beat them to it, with no problem or drama. They had simply looked at each other and *poof*, she was pregnant. It was not so simple for Claire and Neil, and once Claire got off the phone with her friend, after listening to the gush of her friend's ultrasound reports, Claire had had it…game on!

They had books about how to do it, where to do it, and what to do after they did it. They had diets and recipes and magnets and even a few sessions of Claire standing on her head…or at least she tried, until she toppled feet first, landing a kick across Neil's jaw. They both laughed so hard they cried while holding each other, lying naked in the middle of their bedroom.

Months after making the decision to have a baby, the sessions of lovemaking had truly become more robotic and contained more making than love. They knew that their passion for each other was being sucked out of their bedroom, but they knew they had to persevere…at least that's what they thought.

It was Neil's birthday, and they had gone out to their favorite Friday night TexMex restaurant. The salsa, chips, and margaritas flowed, and so did the real, heartfelt conversation about what they had been doing over the last six months. They had decided after the third lime-flavored adult beverage, that neither one of them was really ready to make the next commitment. Neil talked about how he was on the road several days a week selling for the industrial company he worked for, and Claire seemed happy now that she had finally moved into a position of management at the nonprofit. Even though everyone said they needed to have a baby, their lives and actions seemed to be pointing them in a different direction.

"So, what are we saying," Neil asked.

Claire took another sip and doodled her chip through the salsa as a stall tactic. She edged closer to him in the booth and put her head on his shoulder.

"Yea, me too," he said for both of them. "The pressure is just too great to perform. Our friends haven't even lived life as a couple yet. And…" he thought about what he was saying, "…and our parents can just cool their jets about the grandchild thing. When it is our time, God will let us know, and then, well then it will be," he said with a bit of conviction, not really knowing where the sudden clarity came from.

"Yea, I know, right," she said, suddenly full of relief that, without saying it, they had just both agreed to let nature and God's will take its course, and if it was meant to be, well then, it was meant to be.

Neil took a sip of his margarita, also feeling the relief, and missed his mouth, dribbling the ice drink down his chin. Claire laughed at him and reached up with her fingers to wipe it from the five o'clock shadow rounding his chin. Neil reached for the napkin in his lap, but instead his hand found his wife's bare leg and ran his hand up her skirt under the table-clothed booth in the back of the crowded restaurant. From the way she moved closer to him, he knew that everything was okay.

"Can I get you two anything else? Did you save room for desert?" the waiter asked, suddenly standing in front of them.

"Ahhh, no, thanks," Neil said, suddenly blushing like a teenager. "We will get dessert at home." He grinned. "Just the check please."

"We are kind of in a hurry," Claire added with a giggle.

Three weeks later, Neil paced anxiously outside the small master bathroom door; his wife had been in there for about five minutes but it had seemed like thirty!

"Well?"

"Just a minute!"

And that is when the creaky door slowly opened. He was unsure how he could once again comfort the devastation of another failure, and then he looked into those eyes, the eyes that caught him when he was younger, the eyes of the most beautiful woman he had ever seen.

"I don't even need to ask, I can see it on your face!"

"It's positive. We're having a baby!" she said, waving the pregnancy stick in his face. After numerous visits to the doctors, crazy diets, vitamins, and dozens and dozens of sessions of peeing on pregnancy sticks, it had finally happened; it had only taken them giving up the pressure, a great night of joyous sex, and turning it over to God. Neil threw his arm around her, picking her up with a giant spinning hug. He buried his head in her hair, knowing that they truly were blessed.

< >

"Did you think that it would be so simple after that?" The Old Man asked.

Neil looked at the back of the Old Man's head, driving daggers into it. These were his feelings, his memories, and sharing them with the Old Man was not something he enjoyed, not this time.

"Neil," the Old Man turned to look at him with his own passionate blue eyes. "I already know, it is alright to share them with me. Besides, they are part of our journey, and part of the path that we walk." He paused, looking way off along the trail ahead. "This journey is not really about where you have been, but it is very important to where I think you should go. You are more."

Neil stood there, staring at the man. He was unsure of many things, but at that moment, he felt like he had been given a hint of something else. I am more. He felt it was what people feel when they say they felt grace. The sensation washed through him and intensified his thoughts about when Claire was pregnant. He sensed it was important to relive this particular memory; although he didn't yet know why.

"Please, Neil, don't let me keep you from her. I never have, and I never will," the Old Man said, holding his palms open in invitation. "Your life with Claire, it is vital to our relationship. People are put in your path to do many things: to challenge you, to make you angry, to force you to achieve, to make you fail, and to help you rise again. They are put before you to inspire and motivate and, above all, they are put there to help you have a meaningful life that is full of passion. Claire is that person to you," the Old Man said with a smile and a nod. "Please tell me more."

Neil closed his eyes, looking to grab onto the strength of the vibrant memory. He knew that it was important that he remembered these events: He knew it was important for people to be put in front of him, but both things were still mysteries as to why.

< >

Five months into the pregnancy, Neil was staying in a Nashville hotel, prepping for a meeting with one of his biggest automotive accounts. He was putting the finishing touches on the PowerPoint slide deck for the following day's presentation when the hotel phone rang. It was at that second that he realized that he had left his bag phone in the car. He was ready to yell at the front desk staff for calling him so late, when he realized that the desperate voice on the other end of the line was his wife; and she was not well.

"Neil, I need help," her voice trailed off weakly.

< >

"What did you feel when you received that call?" the Old Man asked.

Neil dragged his foot along the path, moving the dirt lightly, and avoiding the answer in his mind. "Helplessness," he whispered.

"I would agree," the older man said, matter of factly. "Remember that feeling, for I want you to see it in others. For when you can recognize the helplessness of another man, and you have the power to help, you will be acting on my behalf and with my authority."

Neil raised an eyebrow at the Old Man, before the power of the memory overtook him again.

< >

"Neil, I can't keep anything down, I am so sick...I am so weak, I don't know what to do."

"Honey, look, ahhh," Neil rubbed his forehead with his other hand, wishing for a Star Trek–like teleporter to beam him to his wife, nearly four hours away.

"I haven't felt the baby in a long time. I'm really worried!"

"Jesus help us! How long has it been?"

"I don't know, most of the day."

"Oh dear God," Neil whispered while covering the phone. "Look, it'll be okay...ahh...call your mom. I know she is thirty minutes away, but I am nearly four hours, and I am leaving now, so call her and go to the hospital. I am leaving now. I love you."

"I love you too. Hurry!"

< >

"Do you remember driving to get to her?"

"I...I do...kind of." Neil's vision seemed to blur as he thought about the memory from so many years ago. "I know I got in my truck and drove. There were no cops, no traffic, no nothing. I hit Atlanta traffic just before the crunch and met her at the hospital just a few hours after she had been admitted."

Twenty-four hours later he was wheeling her out of the hospital, still pregnant, but better.

"What happened after that?"

"After that, I watched her like a hawk, but…"

"But what?"

"It was not two weeks later before our life truly changed."

"Do you know how important that extra few weeks were to your son's development?"

Neil looked at him with the tilted head of someone with many questions before the experience washed over him again.

<>

"Don't leave me!"

"I'm not going anywhere."

Neil had met his wife for lunch, and had agreed to go with her to her OB appointment; even though he had a load of preparation work to do before the start of a local trade show.

The doctor was moving the new hi-resolution ultrasound wand through the squish of KY jelly to reveal that not only did they have a baby in distress, but they had also lost one of the babies along the way that no one had really known was there. It was time to take the last one out, or risk losing that one as well.

"Do you want to know…you know," the doctor said, without thinking, "just in case."

Claire looked at her husband and he at her. Their souls were connected, and the hurt and worry that poured out of Neil's eyes into his wife's spoke volumes. He gently thumbed the tear away from the crease of his wife's eye. They both answered, without looking at the doctor…

"Yes."

"It's a boy."

An hour later, Claire had been admitted to the emergency room and was being prepped for surgery. Neil called everyone that he could think to call. Their parents were in the waiting room and their best friends were en route, but as Neil watched his wife wheeled off on the hospital gurney, he felt the weight of the world on his shoulders and he was alone. He had been issued green scrubs to wear into the surgical room; so with no further support from anyone, he donned them, and smiled for the first time in a while, as he realized that he still wore cowboy boots. He decided to keep them on, flipping the scrub shoes aside.

"Mr. Abrams, it's time," a petite nurse said to him and led him to a bench outside of the surgery room. Satisfied that he would sit on the bench, the nurse entered the surgical room, leaving him alone again, but not without taking a second glance at the cowboy boots that protruded at the end of the green scrubs. She smiled, and it showed, even though she wore a surgical mask.

Neil had often been considered moderately popular. He rarely lacked for friends, and when he entered a room he never found it difficult to strike up a conversation with most anyone standing around. Although not the life of the party, he was usually near the center of attention. But today, sitting on the bench, under the antiseptic hum of the florescent lighting, he felt that he was the last person on earth...the ultimate wallflower. He could sense that everything he held dear—everything that he loved—Claire, was on the other side of the double swinging doors. But, the other side of the doors might have been ten thousand miles away from where he was right now. He was alone...and that is when he decided to do something that he usually left to his wife, he lowered his head in prayer.

Neil closed his eyes, letting the quiet of the space envelope him. "Dear Lord, please forgive me for the sins that I have committed and those that I will commit," he said softly. "Please Lord, my wife and our baby…a boy…a son, a son just like you have…are in there," he felt the first tear fall from his face and splash on the tile floor. "I just want you to be with them and make them safe."

"Hey, are you okay?" Neil looked up to see a tall man in scrubs ask. Without invitation he took a seat on the bench next to Neil. The man was masked, but it was his eyes—like two blue marbles perched above the horizon of the mask—that Neil locked onto. They were like blue pools of mercy, each surrounded by bushy brown eyebrows. Neil could see the creases on his head push together from a smile, as he seemed to know that Neil acknowledged his presence. He had no name on the chest of his scrubs like the other doctors and nurses. He simply smiled.

"Yea, I think," Neil mustered. The lanky man nodded, still smiling.

"You know I have been through thousands of these," the lanky man said, nodding at the double door.

"Yea?"

"Yea."

"So…well…how do they go?" Neil said, grateful for the chatter to give him something to hold on to.

"Most turn out just fine, and in your case, I think that your wife and your son are going to do very well," the man said, putting his hand on Neil's knee. "You need to have faith," he said, standing and moving toward the double door.

"Wait!" Neil said, stopping him from pushing the doors open.

"Yes."

"Are you sure they'll be alright?"

"Neil, I am very sure. Let's talk later, alright!" And with that, he pushed through the doors, leaving Neil alone.

A few seconds later, the petite nurse came out of the same doors to help him scrub and glove and then take him into the room, but she stopped short of Neil, looking down at his feet—the cowboy boots—and then giggled through her mask at him. "Come on cowboy, let's go help your wife have a baby," she said, ushering him into the small room and into a position alongside the head of his wife.

"I told them not to start until you got here!" Claire said, prepped for surgery, with tubes in her arm, her head taped down to the bed and a medical screen dividing her view from what was about to happen to her abdomen. "I am so scared," she whispered.

Neil stroked her hair; he could feel the perspiration on her forehead, and see the fear of the unknown in her eyes. "I am too, but they know what they're doing. The doctor told me you're going to be okay."

"And our baby?"

Neil nodded before answering, the knowledge from the tall lanky doctor giving him hope. "And our baby, our son, he will be okay, too," he said comforting both of them.

"All right Claire, I am starting now," the surgeon said, looking over the screen to catch her eyes. "Claire, you are going to feel a lot of pressure, okay?" Neil looked at the doctor and listened to the voice, and realized that *she* was not the bushy blue-eyed doctor that he had just talked to in the hall. He quickly looked around, and except for the short plump anesthesiologist, the other four people in the surgery room were all female.

Claire nodded, and the surgery began. "Oh…" she moaned sixty seconds into the procedure. "I don't think I can do this. I'm going to be sick!"

"You can't do that Claire." Came the reply from the doctor on the other side of the screen. "Your stomach is on your chest. Dr. Calvin, push the first half," she ordered the anesthesiologist, who immediately thumbed half of a syringe into the tube connected to Claire's arm.

"What's that?" Neil asked anyone who would listen, but they all ignored him.

"I will do…" Claire said, before her speech trailed off and her eyes rolled to the back of her head. The narcotic making short work at smothering her senses.

"Baby's out," the surgeon said, handing the three-pound baby over to one of the nurses.

"I have the baby," the nurse said, moving him quickly to a separate exam table.

Neil watched the commotion that now surrounded the baby…his son.

"Okay Mr. Abrams, per our earlier discussion and the paperwork that you signed, I am going to sever the fallopian tubes and cauterize them so that the baby factory is officially shut down. Okay?" Neil looked at her, but never really heard what she was saying. He was looking past her, at the backs of the three medical people, all working on his son. "Mr. Abrams, is that correct?" Neil looked up at the doctor, who was holding a tool that resembled an industrial soldering iron, and nodded. The doctor then put her head down to seal the deal and close up her patient. She had seen hundreds of fathers in this early stage of shock: just another day in the Baby ER!

Neil stood, his legs wobbly. He looked at Claire, her eyes were closed and there was no sign of comfort on her face. She had no idea he was standing there, or which way was up or that she had just had a baby ripped out of her. He started moving around the table toward where his son was being worked on. There was no noise. *Aren't babies supposed to make noise? Aren't they supposed to cry?*

One of the nurses saw him coming and moved aside so that he could see. The baby was no larger than a small Raggedy-Ann doll, and looked like it came from another world. He thought of all of the babies that he had seen on TV; pink skin, smiling, ready to grab a rattle from your hands and play a game of catch, but this one was different. He had red wrinkly skin and looked more like a red potato after it has been microwaved. His hands were too small for a normal human, and Neil thought he saw an extra digit. Two people in scrubs lifted the baby up and swaddled him in a blanket. They then stood in front of Neil with the small bundle of joy.

"Do you want to hold him before we take him to the NICU?"

Neil looked at the small pound of flesh wrapped in the soft blanket. He felt guilty because he didn't feel a connection yet. "Let's see if Mom wants to be the first to hold him?" he said, avoiding the feelings. And that is when his son made his first sound.

Claire heard it, too, even in her dazed state, her eyes opened and focused long enough to meet Neil's, and a tear rolled down the side of her face. He guided the nurse with the baby to her side.

"You did it honey. You did it, I am so proud of you," Neil said leaning in to nuzzle next to her face. "I love you."

"I love…I love…," she tried speaking, but the narcotic was taking hold again, and pulling her into some calm village in her mind. She was fighting it.

"Would you like to hold your son?" the nurse asked while placing the infant in the crook of her arm and against her breast. Claire smiled as a tear rolled down her cheek.

Neil knelt down next to them and gently touched them both at the same time. He felt his own tears fall off his cheek.

< >

"There are not many things in life that are more beautiful than the creation of life," the Old Man said, a bit misty-eyed himself, as he sat listening to Neil's story. "You will never grow tired of the wonder of love being born." Neil nodded like he understood the deep wisdom of what the man was speaking about.

"So, who was he?" Neil shocked himself by asking the question. "The one with the eyes." He knew he should be wrapped up in the birth of his son, but in retelling the story, he had realized that there was someone there that was divinely unaccounted for. Someone that he had never really questioned before.

"The tall doctor I presume," the Old Man said, cocking his head back a bit with a self-gratifying smile.

"That's the one. He wasn't in the room. He wasn't anywhere. And there was only one way in or out."

The Old Man seemed to think about where the conversation had turned. He was pleased at the younger man's perception, but he knew that he still had much to learn about this journey. "He was watching over you…all of you," the Old Man finally said.

"Watching over me…" Neil's voice trailed into a whisper.

"Son, it is safe to say that there are some mysteries that are best left undiscovered, and sometimes it is just better to accept what is happening rather than trying to understand why it is happening."

"He said we would talk again."

The Old Man took his tin-rimmed glasses off to look squarely at the young man before speaking. "And so you have."

CHAPTER 7

"Is this whole thing a test?"

"Is what a test, Neil?"

Neil looked up the trail, toward the top of the mountain. The sun had moved to behind them, casting elongated shadows of the trees in the valley, but it was also illuminating the peak in front of them; like a beacon, calling them toward its radiance. The path that the Old Man had been leading them on was taking them out of the valley, away from the river, and up the other side of the mountain toward the shining mountaintop.

"This," Neil waved his hand around as if to make a point, "all of this…this place, your questions, my stories, what I experience…my emotions…you!"

The Old Man considered his younger companion for a second, also taking the time to look up at the shining mountaintop. "I believe that is a fair question. Yes."

"Yes? Yes, what? What does, 'yes,' mean?"

"Yes means that, yes, this is a test, but, it is not me that is proctoring this test. It is you."

Somewhere along the way, Neil had accepted that he was really with God, taking this walk, having these conversations. But whether he was dead or not still eluded him.

"I don't understand. You brought me here, I am following you on this walk. This is your place," Neil said exasperated.

At the end of a deep exhale, the Old Man had seemed to expect this line of question. "Actually, Neil, this is your journey, and you have invited me along. It is true, that I do some of the heavy lifting from time to time, but at the end of the day, it is your journey, and it is your belief in me that has brought us to this point. As for this place," he paused to look around as Neil had a moment earlier. "This place is your place. It represents your journey, your triumphs, your failures, your happiness, and your fears. I am honored to be a big part of it all."

Neil nodded. He could feel in his heart that everything the Old Man was saying was true. The analytical side of his brain had believed that this—everything about this experience—was of his own mind. But just because it was analytically accurate did not mean that it was true. God existed. He had created the universe, the earth, and him. To have an experience with God did not need to be analytically correct. Did it? "But you said I was giving myself the test, I don't understand that part?"

"I have not called you here to take a test. I have called you here to find your love, your passion, understand that grace has always been around you and to encourage your servitude. You know this, and have turned it into a test. Which is fine with me, as you should have all of the answers when the time comes for you to make the decision." The Old Man ended abruptly and started walking slowly up the path.

Neil closed his eyes tightly, he wanted to concentrate, find a way to see what God was asking of him, but his logic wasn't allowing it. He could hear something, something that he thought he had heard a few times on the walk…a whisper in the wind, a quiet breath asking him to decide. *It's a question. It's my question. You want me to see all this stuff, to relive these things to answer a question.* With barely more than a whisper, his lips formed words. "Stay."

"I already know my answer," he said audibly. "I already know my answer," he called after the man. "Wait! I want to stay."

The older man, now a good twenty yards up the trail, stopped. Neil could see him draw in a very deep breath, and the trees seemed to respond by swaying to the rhythm of the man's breathing. He turned around, and Neil squared to meet his gaze. He was sure that he was making a decision that would please the older man.

"Son," the man started, "it is not that simple. Service never is, and the decision to serve is never easy."

"But," Neil sputtered, as he started walking toward the older man. "I have seen so many things. I *am* devoted to you; I will do anything that you ask. I am here." He stopped inches from the man, tears forming in his eyes. "I am here."

The Old Man put his hand on Neil's shoulder. "Son, I know you would do anything that I ask of you, but I am not asking you to do something. I desire gratefulness, not sacrifice, humbleness, not blind abandonment. So, before I really ask you the question you think I am going to ask, we need to courageously finish this journey. Yes?"

Crushed, Neil nodded and then obediently moved off in the direction that he thought they should go. He kicked a small stone forward and let his mind wander to a place that he had locked away as the small stone tumbled down the path. *I do want to serve…courageous huh…Does he think I am scared? I can be courageous.*

< >

Neil stood across the desk of the man in the black robes. On either side of Neil were two men in suits and each holding a legal pad. Neil could hear the man in the robe, the family court judge, speaking to him, but at thirteen years of age, he found it hard to concentrate on what exactly his words meant. Weariness and confusion ran rampant through his body and infested his mind.

Neil had spent most of the night in deep discussion with his mother and stepfather. He had not been allowed to see his father and stepmother the morning before the proceedings. He was incredibly tired and very…very scared. The process of custody, something that should have been worked out years earlier, was now put squarely on the shoulders of a thirteen-year-old boy. Fear and confusion—these were the two emotions he had. But it was with these two emotions that he found refuge, these two emotions were making him strong, and gave him the ammunition to fight off the real emotion that he needed to keep down: disappointment.

As the man in the black robes spoke about legal issues and rights of each of the parents, Neil never thought to ask about his rights; he just wanted to run. He wanted to hide. He wanted to go back to his home, get his dog, and just be done with it all. At his grandfather's farm, he could let his dog run free to chase the cows while he pierced greasy fat-back with the barb of a hook and tried his luck with a cane pole against some of the heaviest brim he had ever caught.

The reality of the situation was that somewhere deep inside he knew that his dog, the farm, the fish, and the cows lumbering in the field were all a dream. As much as he tried to stop the terror from eating him up, he knew that in that same place where the dream was hatched, that place somewhere deep inside, the dream clawed to evolve into a nightmare; and he knew…he knew, that for this to end, the dream and the nightmare, he would have to make the decision of who got custody.

He was so scared, he was so confused; he was worn down. Strange thoughts worked their way into his imagination about the outcome; about what would happen if he made the *wrong* decision. What would his mother think; what would she do? What would his father think, a man that had been largely absent in his life? Would he be disappointed in him, too? What would the two people that always accepted him for who he was, his grandmothers, do, now that one of them would possibly never get the chance to hold him again? This was life, his life he was considering. But sadly, he was thinking about everyone's life but his own. Perspective should not be so deep for children so young.

What had started out as a challenge by his biological father to see his son more often had turned into an all-out war of legal eagles, empty threats, and a decision that would alter the life of one boy for decades. Neil often reflected on the decision as an adult; as he watched his children grow, he knew they derived benefits and losses from the decision that he made as a thirteen-year-old. His decision impacted multiple generations, up and down the line. As an adult, he knew that he should have never been allowed to be put in that position, let alone, make a decision of such magnitude.

As a boy, Neil had tried to consider everything; people had often remarked at how grown up he always seemed. Little did they know that he had been forced to grow up, to act like an adult, to take responsibility. His father reappeared in his life on an unpredictable schedule, his time in Vietnam robbing him of a meaningful relationship with Neil or his mother. So, somewhere between being put on an airplane alone by one parent and being picked up by another, Neil had learned to talk to everyone from the flight attendants to the pilots. He didn't want their help. He wanted their respect; and now, standing in the legal chamber, he wanted to shed the respect and have someone else make the decision.

Neil had thought through what his response would be, but he never thought he would be asked. He knew, after living with his mother for most of his life, that he wanted to try the other side of the coin. His father, although unpredictable, was still his father. But, he would also be able to be near the farm, the cow, and the fishing pond. Young boys have vision that is usually very shortsighted, even when they act grown up.

Neil looked at the Judge and saw his mouth moving. He saw the lawyers flip through manila folders and legal pads as they argued, but in the chaos of the legal chamber all he could hear was a steady and empowering voice that comforted him and gave him confidence. It was the voice of his grandmother, his father's mother. Granny Eve had been the lady that protected from one of the most horrific events to happen to him in his short life.

Granny Eve was the true matriarch of the family. Everyone gathered at her house on Sunday after church for lunch. In the regular absence of Neil's father, Granny Eve was the one who offered advice, guidance, and sometimes money to fund dreams.

She was a polished woman on the outside. She built her status with hard work and intelligence, but, with all of her success, she had managed to cultivate a warm and loving presence around her family and friends.

Granny Eve and Granddad had built a small business together. They had seen the need for clean water and sewer, and had purchased the right-of-way along a small military town during the 1940s that allowed them to lay pipe, provide water, and build a customer base. On many occasions, Granny Eve allowed Neil to come to her place of business while Granddad worked the crews in the field, buying more land and laying more water and sewer pipe. It was on one of these occasions, while spending the afternoon at their storefront, that Neil learned the meaning of sacrifice and courage.

Granny Eve had a sign above the business name inside the small office that said *LORD MAKE US COURAGEOUS.* It was from under this sign that Neil would lean around the wall of the brown-carpeted office, as customers would come in to pay their water and sewer bill. Most times, they would write a check, or plop a sum of money down on the counter and walk out with nothing more than a smile. There was one time where this was not the case.

On a January day a week before Neil's tenth birthday, he sat at his little desk, under the sign, penciling in squares on his grandfather's graph paper. The familiar chime of the front glass door opening summoned him to look up. In walked another customer, with another story of why they couldn't pay the bill.

"I need to pay my bill, but I don't got it," Neil heard a gruff-voiced man say to Lewis, the man who had worked with his Granny Eve for nearly twenty years.

"Well," he heard Lewis say as Neil peeked around the corner, catching the first glimpse of the gruff-speaking man. He was wearing a white long-sleeve shirt that was dirty in a way that suggested that it had been on him for several days. His hair was unkempt, but was still short enough to suggest that he might have been military. He kept looking over his shoulder at who else might be coming in the door behind him.

"Lewis, is there an issue?" Neil's Granny Eve asked, rounding the corner and mussing Neil's straight brown hair at the same time.

Both men looked back at the lady in her mid sixties. She was short in stature, small in her shoulders, but she carried her presence with dignity and respect. She was larger than life, mostly stubborn, usually direct, and more often than not got her way; but underneath it all, Neil knew that she was as kind as the day was long. He loved her for her sweet tea, her ability to catch anything on a rod and reel, and that she accepted him, broken parents and all.

"Miss Eve," the gruff man said, obviously recognizing Neil's grandmother. "I didn't know you were here, too?"

"How is your mother doing, Dillon? She is working over at the mill these days, right?" she asked, ignoring his question, and disarming a situation that she had dealt with hundreds of times before.

The gruff man, Dillon, was slightly taken back by her directness. He still looked surprised that she was in the office.

"Ahh, she's fine ma'am, she finally settled with that Jonesy man…" his voice tapered off and he fidgeted with his pockets while looking at the floor. "You know I am good for it, the bill I mean. But…but the base ain't pay'n no more," he said quickly, while seeing the child for the first time. Their eyes locked for an instant. Even at almost ten, Neil knew pain when he saw it in a man's eyes. He had seen it in his father's eyes the few times that he had actually seen him.

"Really?" she said, trying to maintain total control of the situation. She watched him slowly pivot his stare back to her. "I have heard that they've stopped all the benefits for now. That's too bad. Have you been working with your commander?" she asked, all the while her hands slowly reaching under the front counter.

"That's right, they aren't no help neither. Damn fools!" Dillon said, finding the point of anger very rapidly. "And now I can't pay for the water, the rent, my old lady's food, beer, or nothing." He looked over his shoulder again, past the glass door; there were no other customers coming in.

"Look, I can let this month go," Granny Eve said, opening a small drawer and producing a twenty-dollar bill. "Here," she handed the money over and put it squarely in his hand while looking up into his eyes. She held the stare while holding his hand. "Go back to the base and talk to your commander again. Tell them I sent you. I know you can deal with this, now get out there and show the Lord that you are courageous and worth his grace. I believe in you and what all you boys were doing over there." She simply shut his hand and nodded toward the door. "We will see you next month with the what you can manage…okay?"

Dillon looked at his clinched hand and then at the open drawer of money. He then looked back up at Granny Eve and then again at the boy sitting on the floor.

The first gunshot was so quick that Neil never realized what was happening. In a flash of hate, mistrust, and confusion, Lewis flew backward against the wall, his blood splattering Neil's face, freezing him to the spot. Granny Eve somehow knew what to expect and had pulled a pistol from under the counter and fired. The glass door exploded and fell to the floor like pellets of ice. Granny's round had missed, or went right through the man.

Dillon moved with speed and cunning that can only be learned in combat. He turned the gun toward Neil and vaulted the counter in one swift move.

< >

"That man was very troubled," the Old Man said, knitting the wrinkles on his brow together with a look of concern and worry.

Neil, unaware that he had been talking at all, slowly let his focus come back to the older man sitting across from him. "I was so scared."

"I know you were son," the Old Man said taking a second to collect his thoughts. "Would you believe me if I told you that this, all of this, all of that...it is all part of my plan?" He let the words hang on the air. "Your Granny Eve, based on all of her experiences and all of the trials and tribulations that she had been through...her experiences from the path that she was walking on, prepared her for that moment...that moment where she sacrificed her love to protect you."

< >

The boy of almost ten years of age, with no more than life itself to live for, froze in the deepest pool of fear as the man vaulted the counter with the barrel of his gun pointing right at his face. For Neil, the seconds slowed down to a visual picture that would always be etched on his soul.

The man, still in mid vault, fired his second shot. Neil could see the squeeze of the finger. He could hear the ratcheting of the chamber as it spun to load the next round, and he could sense the action of the hammer as it pulled back for its blow...and then he saw what he thought were angels, but in reality, it was the small stature of his grandmother trading her soul for that of her grandson. The shot fired, and she fell to the ground crumbling her body around the boy in a desperate surge of protection.

With the shot fired, the man put his free hand on the cash till and then paused, his feelings catching up with his actions. Guilt—gut squeezing guilt—struck him like a sledgehammer. Instead of success, he felt pain—real pain—agonizing pain as the blood trickled down his arm from Granny Eve's first shot. The blood pooled onto the crisp bills; the paper sucked in the color, turning the green to black. Dillon looked at the pool of blood in the till and traced his fingers in small circles, his mind thinking of other places he had seen blood. He lifted a few of the bloody twenties to his face crumpling them against his eyes trying to stop the pain of what he had just done. Large sobs erupted, pushing past the bills and mixing with blood to trace along the creases of the bills and fall as pink splotches on the floor.

And as one of the tears fell, the seconds that had been running in slow motion started ticking faster.

The man stood above the boy, one hand pointed the pistol at Neil's face, and the other held the crumpled dollars to his head. His eyes darted around. He saw the lifeless body of Lewis floating in a circular pool of shiny blood. He saw the carnage of the little lady sprawled across the boy. He saw the tears of a boy roll down a smooth cheek. He felt the pain and the hate and the anger of everything that had happened to him…and he cried into the bills harder.

Neil looked down at his grandmother. She was not breathing, or talking or telling anyone that they could be better. He looked up at the man.…and that is when he heard him pull the hammer back on the gun.

The man with the gruff voice, the man that was so angry…Dillon, pulled the bills from his face, his own blood leaving splotched red tattoos like barbwire across his forehead…and with that he seemed to realize what he had just done. He looked away from the carnage and up at the sign above the doorway—LORD MAKE US COURAGEOUS—and sighed, gently closing his eyes and whispering something that only he could hear.

Dropping the wad of wet bills in a lump on the floor, his head slowly leaned forward as he looked down at Neil; the crumpled kid protected by his eighty-five–pound grandmother. Dillon smiled at the boy just before he put the gun to his own head and pulled the trigger.

< >

"I was so scared."

"I know you were son, I was there with you."

Neil sat quietly. He had grown used to the movement between reliving his past and understanding that God had been with him every step of the way…but it had made him weary, and every time he wanted to know about what was happening today, the Old Man found a way, a question, a vision, a memory to allow him to relive a point of relevance from his past. Neil knew that this memory—this event—had relevance to what God was now asking him, but, he still had not discovered the meaning.

"What did he say to you?"

The Old Man pushed his brow together and nodded his head up and down slightly as if to say, "Good, you are getting this aren't you."

"He simply asked me for forgiveness."

Neil, too, nodded his head, still trying to unravel the formula of the event that had taken the life of his grandmother and shaken his family so. They both looked at each other in deep thought.

"Did you give it to him?"

CHAPTER 8

The pair walked on the trail for quite some time in silence before the Old Man decided it was time to talk again.

"Part of what I want you to do is to live your life so that it doesn't control you," the Old Man said, bending down to pick up a perfectly sized walking stick.

Neil chewed on that statement for a minute before feeling the need to defend his position. "But, living a life that doesn't control you is not that simple!"

"Sure it is," the Old Man continued. "Your schedules, your rules, your time tables, your conference calls…you put too much into these."

"I should put more into you," Neil whispered, getting it quietly; and actually hearing it for the first time. "But…"

"But what Neil," the Old Man said, stopping the man's doubts before they crossed his lips, yet again. "Let me guess: these things, your schedules, your emails, your cell phone, your devotion to this job of yours—they all enable you to serve me. Right?"

Neil cocked his head a little, allowing the phrase to happily play along with the fantasy of life that he had been leading. "I think so," he muttered in a less than audible tone.

"You think so…hmmm." The Old Man picked up a small stone, turned from Neil, tossed it into the air, and swung at it with the stick. The rock sailed out of sight.

For the first time on their journey, Neil felt ashamed. His mind told him that what he did, his job, allowed him to serve God, but his heart betrayed him.

"Don't let the conflict consume you, son," the Old Man said, his back still to the younger man.

"Then what should I do?"

The Old Man turned around slowly as he started to speak. "I don't want you to ever stop doing what you love. I don't want you to not provide for your family. I don't want you to ever not follow your passion. I do not want you to ever feel that my love can only come at the expense of your career."

"Then what do you want?"

"There is an expression that so many people listen to over my word. They are told by commercials, newspapers, and even their parents, to follow the money." He paused to let that sink in. "I have never said that. I simply want man to follow me, and to love one another," the Old Man said, looking him dead in the eye. "That is it," he said holding his out arm.

Neil never heard the last part, as his mind started challenging the first statement about following the money. *Was it true? Is this who he had become?* He recounted the multiple times he had jumped jobs for better money. Each time he went to the greener pasture, he cut a little piece of his joy away from who he was. Each move placed him just a little bit farther away from his passion; and ultimately, each move consumed something, and took him a little farther away from what God had intended him to do.

"Man needs its processes and it currencies to function. I am not denying that. But what I am saying is that more often than not, as man gets deeper into these processes and its currency, he finds that I am less and less evident." The Old Man said the last bit with a tinge of sorrow in his voice, and then picked up another stone for his next home-run swing.

"Money makes things happen," Neil said, watching the impromptu batting practice.

"Son, that is where you are wrong. People make things happen. Love makes things happen. Passion makes things happen. The joy of serving others makes things happen. You see, people have ideas, and they act on them. They form groups and they respond to issues. A child in the street that has nothing cannot hug a dollar bill and expect the dollar bill to fill his heart."

"But it can help fill his stomach," Neil countered.

"Yes, yes, I suppose it could. But who is going to have the human decency to allow a child like that into their store. And who is going to help that child with their purchase. And who is going to point to the letters on the side of the soup can and read to that child that this is what they need to put in the stomach. And who...," he stopped as the emotion of every poor child in the world that fit that mold seemed to know that He was talking about them, and they all seemed to cry out for His help.

"I am," Neil whispered.

"You will," he said regaining composure. "But it will be with the gifts that I give you. Everyone receives my gifts, and they come in many forms. They are your talents, your passion, your love, and your choices to use them. I find joy in those that use their passions to help others. Each of my passions has a basis of love." He held the stick up to check its beauty and smudged his thumb across the marks left by the stone before speaking again; he seemed to be mulling something over, and the stick only bought him the time necessary to collect his thoughts. "I want to teach you a little about passion and what love can do. I want you to really know this point, it is important, but I can't just tell you, I want you to see it firsthand. This will be a different experience for you," he said, taking the stick and swooshing the dust around his feet into a puff of dust that grew instantly into a larger and larger cloud with each circle of the stick. The cloud of dry clay and rocks bellowed to biblical proportions, rising higher than the trees and blocking out the view of the sun or of Neil's hands in front of him. Fear gripped Neil tightly.

Neil crunched on the grit circling his head; the taste was oily and stale as he spat to keep it from covering his tongue. He shielded his face with his arm, trying not to breath, but the thickness of the dust filled his mouth regardless. Everything he did only seemed to let more dust in—into his eyes, into his ears, and into his clothes. He held his breath, trying not to breathe in, but it was not possible. He coughed hard, racking his body and rubbing his eyes, which only made it worse. *What was the Old Man doing?*

He put his head down to his chest, covering his head, and waited, not breathing, not looking, not doing anything, but waiting for the dust to settle…and ultimately, it did. When he finally opened his eyes, without rubbing them, he realized that he was not where they just were. He was no longer standing on the path, but was now sitting—sitting—in the middle of several old tires…covered in red dust. With a few more racking coughs, he was finally able to take in a lungful of air, and nearly wretched. The stench of rotting trash was overwhelming. Confusion and pain filled his head and consumed his body. The cough had hurt him deeply, and he felt a deep pain like none he had ever experienced. He was so confused and…and…hungry. Oh, dear God, he was more hungry than he had ever experienced. He felt the pain of starvation gripping his dust-covered body.

"Did you find anything?" someone asked him from outside of the tires.

Before he could crane his head over the three tires to turn and look at the questioner, a diesel truck roared by within inches of where he sat, spewing another cloud of dust and fumes over him. He coughed again. *The pain…the hunger.*

"Your cough is getting worse," he heard the person from outside the tires speak again. The voice was small and gentle, almost angelic, and tingled with love and concern.

Neil, still not completely understanding where he was, or why he was here, turned. Behind him, sitting in the oily mud, something that can only be formed by decaying trash, was a little girl of four or five years of age. She was filthy. Her hair, possibly jet-black at one time, was caked in filth, and stuck to her head like pasty cement and dirt. Her lips were cracked, and her skin, covered in sores, hung from her arms nearly exposing her bones. Flies buzzed happily around her, and she paid them no attention. The rags she wore were not more than a pair of old boys shorts that she had messed in at least a few times, and her shirt, which had been blue when she found it, was now no more than a brown sack cloth with no left sleeve.

"What did you say?" Neil said, completely confused. *Why am I here? What are you showing me?*

"Your cough—" another truck rolled by, spewing dirt over them again "—it is getting worse." And with that she went back to scrounging for food around her area.

Neil barely processed that the girl was speaking Spanish, and that he had spoken to her in the same tongue. He tried to stand up from inside the tires, but his legs did not have the strength to push him up and over the three tires. For the first time, he looked down at what he was.

"You should move," she said without looking up, and cutting through the shock of what Neil was experiencing. He was not an observer of this unforgivable situation; he was actually one of the children in this unforgivable situation.

"Oh God, what have you done?" Neil whispered, now trying to push himself out of the ring of tires.

"I told you not to get into those," the girl said, standing from her pile of sludge to help him out of the three tires at the side of the road. "Give me your hands," she said reaching into the tires to pull her seven-year-old brother out of the mess he had gotten himself into. He was all that she knew…all that she had.

Pablo had told her stories of their mother; mostly about when she was sick, or that she could find the best places to hide from the rain. She died in one of those hiding places, burrowed in an old storm drain. She just never woke up, and Pablo had taken care of his sister ever since.

Nince did not know life without her brother, and except for a few broken memories, she had never known life away from the sewers and the trash that others cast off. Nince had no concept that she was the castoff of the castoffs. She could never know that she and her brother were at the final threads of the tapestry of society: The threads that are most often pulled out and tossed to the ground. In the second poorest country in the Western hemisphere, a couple of kids that teetered at the precipice between a pile of trash and the side of the road was normal.

"Give me your hands," she said again.

Neil, put aside what he was, he put aside the stabbing pains of hunger that he felt in every fiber of his small body, and he put aside all doubt of why God had put him in this situation as he reached out for the outstretched hands of the young girl.

What Neil did not sense or feel was that the tower of tires in the pile of trash next to a road in the Central American country of Honduras was about to topple over into the dirt road that they lived next to.

A quarter mile up the road, a white diesel Toyota van was making its way along the same road, oblivious to what lay ahead. You see, on the side of Honduran roads, people walk their goats, they wash their clothes, they farm their crops, they take their baths, they build their huts, and often, the children that have no parents find their way there to scrounge on the discards of cars that drive by without a second thought.

The little girl felt the fragile hands of her brother and squeezed his fingers together trying her best to lift him out of the tires.

Neil stepped on the side of the second tire, flopping his empty belly onto the top tire in time to watch Nince loose her grip and fall backward into the mud-hued street. She froze looking at her brother, then her head turned toward the van headed toward her.

"¡Oh, Dios no!" Neil shouted, pushing his weight, and that of the tires, onto their side and rolling into the street.

The van driver had been chatting lightly with his passengers; missionary people from the United States. They seemed nice enough, a lady and her teenage son: They always seemed nice. They had just visited one of the orphanages' secondary schools and were headed back to the primary school in the city. The director of the school was riding in the passenger seat, also chatting with the

Americans, when, out of the corner of her eye, she saw the tires and the child fall into the road directly in front of them. "*Alto!*" she screamed.

Neil felt the impact of the tower of tires break one of his ribs as he hit the ground, but in the same motion his hands reached the hands of his sister, and with his own frail body, he covered her with what was left of his body. The van stopped with the front tire coming to rest against his back.

The silence of the next few seconds felt like hours. Neil/Pablo could hear nothing but the faith that his sister put in him. His breathing had stopped as he held his breath against the impact of the van and that of the pain from the broken rib creeping up his side.

"Pablo, are we in heaven?" his sister asked him while in his embrace. "I think we are, because I know you will be there to protect me," she said, burying her head a little deeper into his filth-covered chest.

"Children, oh dear God help me help them," Neil heard a woman say just before he was picked up from in front of the van.

"Don't leave me," the girl screamed as her brother was wrenched from her arms.

"Niño, it is okay, you will be okay, God has you," the woman said, lifting him up. "Claire come help me," she yelled to the van in English.

Neil/Pablo released his sister, his mind swirling with what had just happened. "God will protect you," he said to her as he was being pulled away. She looked up at him; fear swirling around the pools of her large brown eyes.

The woman, Claire, a blond American, walked past Neil in child form and gently bent down to talk to the small girl on the ground. Neil could hear that her Spanish was not precise, but with her warm smile and her gentle character, she calmed the girl down, and with no more than outstretched hands she picked the girl up and held her like she had never been held.

The school director, the woman that was holding Neil, was instructing the driver that they needed to get a doctor as soon as possible. It was at that moment that another American stepped out of the van. A young man of sixteen or seventeen years of age walked up to the director and held out his arms. "Let me take him," he simply said, offering no argument against his suggestion.

Neil felt the pain in his side, he felt the hunger in his stomach, he felt the fear in his heart for the little girl, but when he was passed to his son—his actual son—his soul felt God's smile.

Pablo and his sister accepted the warm embraces of the strangers as they were both put into the van. Neil, as Pablo, looked over at his sister. He could see the reflection of the trash heap in her eyes as she watched the only home that she knew move out of her sight. She buried her head in the American woman's shirt and sobbed quietly. A small tear ran down the woman's face and landed on Nince's cheek. The woman wiped it away with her thumb, leaving the only clean spot on the girl's body.

"What is your name, buddy?" the American boy asked Neil gently. He spoke in American-accented Spanish.

"Pablo," Neil said, his voice hoarse, and he coughed and then reached for his side in pain.

"Careful with him Josh, I think he might have a broken rib or two," the director said; a veteran angel for children that have been cast aside.

"Do you want some water?" the American boy asked Neil.

Neil, through the eyes, ears, and touch of a boy from the cesspool of a mound of trash piled at the side of a road, was feeling the very real and warm touch of love...the touch of God...through the hands of his own real-life son. He began to cry. The tears flowed freely, for Neil knew what the boy, Pablo, had been through. In the few minutes that he had been allowed to be a part of Pablo's life, he had felt every painful experience, every sadness, and every doubt that the young boy had ever ingested. But, at the same time, he felt extremely honored and humbled to be a part of love's rescue, to feel God's almighty power come through the gentle touch of an American boy who looked as different from Pablo as black is to white.

"Hey buddy," Josh said, thumbing the tears away from the dirty boy's face, "everything is going to be alright now. You don't need to worry." He stared down at the small Honduran boy; his hair was matted in clumps, and something sticky was along his right side. He wore no shoes and the shorts that he had on seemed much too large. They where held up by a rubber strap lashed around his waist. Josh looked over at his mother; she was rocking the small girl, singing to her gently. The little girl had a grip around her neck and did not look like she would ever let go. Tears formed at the rims of Josh's eyes as the weight of the moment washed over him, and that is when the small boy on his lap moved the tear away with his thumb.

Josh looked at the small boy with a smile that said everything was going to be all right, as the van rolled onto another dirt road and a new cloud of filthy dust rolled through windows.

< >

Neil struggled to catch his breath as he shook his head and coughed from the dust. He rubbed his eyes and without having to open them, knew that he was back…back on the path…back where he had been with the Old Man.

The dust settled like it had never happened, and with little ceremony, the Old Man looked at him, large stick still in his hand, and cocked his eyebrow, as if to say, "Well?"

Neil was overcome with emotion. He had no idea what to say. He simply sat there sucking in racked breaths in-between sobs. He vaguely felt the presence of the Old Man sit down next to him and put his arm around his shoulders.

"You know son, regardless of how we end this walk together, I wanted you to see that God's love will still burn brightly in your family. As you have seen, grace has always been around you; as a lost child, as a young adult falling in love, as a worried parent with a new baby, and now." He stopped to look down the path, as if he could see the end. "And even now, as you walk with me."

Neil stopped sobbing and wiped the tears off the right side of his face. He too looked down the path, following the direction of the eyes of the Old Man. He had seen so much on his walk. He had relived momentous occasions and gut-wrenching fear, but what he had seen most clearly was that the Old Man, God himself, had been with him his entire life.

"Is it time for me to die?"

The Old Man chewed on that for a few seconds, his eyes still fixed down the path. "I don't think so Neil, but really, it is not up to me."

Neil nodded, internalizing everything again. "It's up to me, isn't it? My own will and all?"

"Yes, son. Yes it is. Free will is strong."

"Is it really that simple?" The question broke the Old Man's trance as he stared off toward the end of the trail.

"No, not really."

"How do you mean?"

"Choices always make things more of a challenge," the Old Man said, standing, brushing off his khakis, and stretching his back.

"What kind of choices?" Neil asked, standing and stretching as well, but as his muscles expanded, he felt a sense of calm and comfort. He sensed that his soul was full of love from his last experience, and he could feel a warmth wash over his body that took every ache and pain, both physically and mentally. He wanted to lock the love and the warmth in a place inside of himself to draw strength from later. He smiled for the first time since starting the walk with the Old Man.

The Old Man started moving toward where he had been staring; his motion beckoned Neil to follow. His stick, once used as a makeshift bat, now became a walking stick, a favorite companion on the path that plunked gently with every other step.

Neil watched him move on before the Old Man stopped and turned.

"You coming?"

Neil, awash with a peaceful glow, nodded and dopily walked along the path, following the man and his stick that plunked.

"What about those choices I have to make?" Neil asked, surprising himself with the question.

The Old Man kept moving, as if he was now on a time schedule.

"I want you to see and feel a few more things before we really start talking about choices."

CHAPTER 9

The pair walked for what seemed like an hour before Neil felt the rush of the last experience slowly ebb like a setting sun. As his mind moved from the acceptance of what can be to the analytical of what should be, he pieced together for the first time what was so glaringly different about the last experience.

"He was older," Neil said under his breath, referring to his son, but still not quietly enough so that the Old Man did not pick up on it. *That was the future.*

"Before I answer that," he stopped and looked at Neil, "because it really was meant to be a question, let me reflect on just how quickly you moved from just accepting the possibility of God's love holding you like a cradle and keeping you safe to the logic of trying to figure it out. Sometimes you just need to accept, to accept the feeling, to feel the grace."

"Ah…" Neil went to speak, but the Old Man put up a finger to stop him.

"Don't think Neil….feel. Feel with your heart. In your daily life you are given glimpses of God's grace, of His love. This is a small window into the bountiful glory of Heaven. Sometimes you see it, and other times it simply passes you by. But sometimes…just sometimes, you get to absorb it and make it a part of your soul." He took his finger and placed it on Neil's heart. "You just had that experience when you met your son…your son that is several years older than he is now." He let that hold in the air for a moment.

"So, I just answered your question…yes…it is an older version of your son, and yes, that was a glimpse into the future and yes, that was a glimpse into the Kingdom of God. Do you have anymore questions?" He turned and put his hand out to touch a wild vine that was dangling from a nearby tree.

"Ahh, no, I don't think so, but...yes I think so," he said, still processing all that was happening.

"Mmm, feel...not think," the Old Man said, now studying the detail of the woody vine.

Neil dug in to hang onto the feelings, but his thoughts kept coming back to one thing, something that he had overlooked, until now. "So she is fine, my wife, Claire. She is okay after...you know, after the accident." His eyes welled again. He was feeling again. A lump formed in his throat when he realized that she and Josh were the only two on the mission trip, and he was not. "Does that mean that I am..."

"Fine you say," the Old Man started, cutting across his words and his train of thought. "Yes, she is fine, but she is changed. She is forever changed after the accident."

Neil lowered his head, his attention falling on the path, the path that held more questions than answers. *It's because I am not there.* "What about me?" Neil said quietly. "Where am I?"

The Old Man tugged gently on the vine, testing its strength and looking up to see what it was attached to. "You are with me," the Old Man simply said.

Neil looked at the man, took a step closer, and spoke. "I am with you? What does that mean, I am with you? Am I dead? I keep asking the same question. I never get an answer." Neil felt anger rise in him like an old friend. "We are walking around on this stupid path. What is this place? Heaven or...what?" He stopped when he realized the Old Man had been holding his words as Neil ramped up. "What?"

"I think you misunderstand me, son."

"What's to misunderstand? You have me here, I want to go there, but for some reason I have no choice in the matter and I am here. How is this God's love?"

The Old Man nodded gently. "You are finally getting around to it," he said, passing the vine to Neil. "You do have a choice."

"What am I to do with this?" he asked, looking at the vine.

"Just take it and hold on," the Old Man said, thrusting it in his hand.

Neil took the vine. It felt as if warm blood was pulsing through the vine. He looked up into the tree, but there was no tree. Instead he saw the hospital white tone of acoustic ceiling tile. He looked back at the Old Man, but instead saw the face of a very old man. His jaw hung open and drool flowed down his unshaven chin. The vine in his hand seemed to bite into his fingers and he looked down at his hands. His hands were frail, but not sickly. He had faded pink rose-colored nail polish on and one of his fingers seemed to be permanently bent like a hook. His frail hands, those of an elderly woman, worked the vine/rope…the rope that was tying her down to the seat.

"Don't fight it honey," a large black woman said, patting her on the knee as she walked by.

Neil, now in the body and soul of an old woman, tugged on the rope again, it was painful to his hands and the rope was tight around his thighs. His feet were cold from the lack of blood. Panic starting gripping him as he looked around for help; but what he saw offered no help, only pain, suffering, and neglect. There was no love in this room. Terror flashed through his brittle system.

The stench of feces in the air was mixed with the caustic odor of disinfectant. He could hear moans and laughter. Suddenly, he was aware that everyone was sitting. Everyone was tied to their own chair. Everyone was old and everyone looked like they were there to die.

"Oh God, what have you done?" He asked aloud and heard the rickety voice of an elderly woman. He looked around for anything that he recognized, anyone that could help him… anything! He started pulling against the ropes, the ropes that bound him to the chair; and that is when he heard a familiar voice. The voice cut through his fear like a lighthouse in the fog.

"Hey Granny, how are you?" the young man asked as he moved across the room and knelt down in front of her. Neil's eyes, the eyes of an old lady, slowly looked up from the ropes. A bruise had started along her fingers from struggling. Her eyes, the eyes of an eighty-eight-year-old woman, through dirty glasses, met the youthful eyes of a young man—his own youthful eyes. He was looking at himself from inside his grandmother: He was looking at a twenty-two-year-old Neil.

"Granny, why are you tied to the chair?" a young woman asked, coming up next to Neil. It was Claire, and she immediately started untying the ropes.

"Nurse." the young Neil stood up, stopping the large black lady. "Why is my grandmother tied to a chair?"

The nurse, oblivious to the condition in which she worked, rounded on the younger man. "Why is she tied to a chair you say?"

Neil moved to answer, but the nurse cut him off.

"She is tied to a chair because she won't take her meds. She is tied to a chair because she's in Brookside, a state run facility. She is tied to a chair because her insurance don't pay for her to go anywhere else but here, and she is tied to a chair…just like the others," she waved her arm around the room, "because there is forty of them and only one of me! They don't pay me enough damn money, and I need them to take their damn meds. That is why she is tied to a chair. Okay?"

Neil swallowed his pride, assessed the situation he was in, and calmly spoke again. "If I get her to take her meds, can I untie her and take her outside?"

The nurse went to speak, but decided to take the help instead. "Here," she put a small cup with two pills in his hand. "Have her back in her room in an hour."

"God bless you," Claire said, still untying the rope.

"God don't have nothing to do with it," the nurse said, still with a tinge of attitude. "Do you think any of these people even know who God is anymore? Look at 'em. Why would God do this to them…or, for that matter, why would He put me here to work with 'em. Honey, God has left the building, and He left me to clean up

His mess." She walked off, handing small cups of pills to people strapped down in chairs. Each person simply opened their mouth and swallowed.

"Neil," Granny said weakly, holding her hand out to touch him.

Neil turned and knelt next to his grandmother again. This was his mother's mother, one of the two great ladies that helped raise him. After Granny Eve was shot, Granny Lilly tried to bring the family back together, but it had been in vain. She would die knowing that her good friend would be on the other side, waiting for her.

Neil took her hand, feeling the warm wet blood meet his fingertips from where she had been tugging with the rope. "Come on Granny Lil, let's get you outside for some fresh air."

Claire and Neil gently helped the elderly matriarch of his mother's family stand up and get her footing. She was frail, and the last few months had not been kind to her. Claire zipped up the front of Granny's green housecoat and pushed her pink slippers securely on her feet. The three then gently navigated through the maze of drugged and dazed elderly people to the doors that led outside.

"I will never forgive them," Claire muttered to Neil quietly, her mouth hard with anger and her eyes red with tears of sadness.

"We'll find a way to fix this," Neil said to his young wife, with an even expression. He was rabid with anger, but he didn't need to show it here and now. He needed to be stable for his grandmother; he needed to be strong for the woman that practically raised him.

The older Neil, through the eyes, body, and soul of his elderly grandmother, knew how this day would end. His younger self would try and administer the medication, a drug that numbed her senses and made her compliant and easy for others to control. It was the same routine for hundred of thousands of elderly people every day, and Granny was caught in the routine. But, today, the younger Neil would never get the chance to give the meds. Today was meant for other things. They were all there for a reason.

Granny Lil knew that God had brought them there for a reason…for a message.

For the first time since Neil had started on the path with the Old Man, he felt that he was beginning to understand what was being asked of him. But also, unlike his last experience while living the life of a homeless boy, this time it was different. He was here, in his grandmother's body, looking through her eyes and feeling her pain, but *she* was here also, allowing him to share her mind and soul; under one condition: that she be allowed to deliver a message.

The fresh air washed over the trio as they walked out of the institution and into the entrance garden. In contrast to the putrid smell and drabness from inside the building, the garden blossomed with beauty and abounded with peaceful fresh air. In one corner stood a stoic Japanese maple; it offered deep shade and a cool sanctuary for reflection. Perched under the tree sat a weathered concrete bench inviting them to sit.

Claire guided Granny Lil to the bench while young Neil fished in his pocket for the meds. Granny Lil touched his hand once he produced the meds, and in a gentle, non-verbal way, asked him to wait. Neil nodded, noting that some of the blood from her hands had left a pattern on his fingers. He moved to help Granny sit on the bench, but stopped as something in the tree caught her eye.

"What do you see Granny?" Claire asked, looking up at the tree.

Granny, with the older Neil temporarily guiding her soul, enjoyed a clarity and respite from the dementia that had plagued her these last few months. This was his opportunity to do what he was brought here to do, and he sensed that Granny knew what he was about to say, and she approved.

In the tree, wedged between a branch and the curve of some bark, stood a small copper cross. No more than three inches in height, the thin earthen metal had oxidized to shades of green and gray. Neil followed his grandmother's eyes up the tree to see the cross. Standing on his toes to get a closer look at the cross, he was surprised she had even seen it hidden in the foliage and at such a height. It had obviously been placed there and forgotten for years, if not generations. He removed the cross and brought it down to the bench.

"It has an inscription," he said, rubbing his fingers across the metal to expose the words; Granny's blood serving as the polish.

"Follow Me," the young Neil said, gently rubbing his thumb across the copper, trying to pull out the shine of the metal.

"Good eyes Granny," Claire said, rubbing the round of Granny's shoulder, and feeling the loose skin and bones of a woman neglected.

"Neil," Granny said, pausing to clear her throat. She had not strung together a clear sentence in months, and it felt liberating.

"Yes, Granny," Neil responded, taking his eyes off of the cross and looking right into her eyes.

"You too Claire," she said, taking the cross from her grandson's hands; which he surrendered without question.

"Yes Granny, what can we do for you?" Claire asked, also noticing a new clarity in her eyes.

"Not me sweetie, you can't do anything for me now, I am talking about you." The older Neil heard his grandmother's mind form the words that he needed to deliver. She cleared her voice again, a voice hoarse from not being used and a pitch that wavered, as older people's voices do.

Claire and Neil exchanged glances across the lady, the grandmother who had raised him like her own, and treated Claire like a daughter.

"I have something for both of you," she started again, smacking her lips dryly. "Before you give me that medicine." She put her hand up to stop Neil's protest. "I want you both to know that God works." She sat quietly for a moment as both of the young adults waited for her to add something in her moment of lucidity.

"How do you mean granny, 'God Works'?" Claire asked gently, once again exchanging a puzzled look with her husband.

"It is right here, in my hand, this cross," she said, running her bony finger across the inscription herself; her own blood deepening the boldness and meaning of the text. "You see, God is coming to take my soul to live with Him soon; I know that, but I also know that he has also given me a great gift."

Young Neil was shocked at the clarity in his grandmother; a flash of fury crossed his face as he seemed to think that this clarity had always been here, and that it was time to get her out of this hellhole.

"My gift is that I am being allowed to talk to you; it is that God is using me…using me now, as His instrument of peace. He is talking through me now, so that you will both understand something."

Young Neil looked over at Claire, small tears had started pooling at the bottom of her beautiful blue eyes and he could see that she was hearing what Granny was saying…she was actually hearing God in her elderly voice.

"Go on Granny," she said squeezing her hand.

"He wants me to tell you that you are both blessed and you are loved, and when you are together your blessings and your love multiply. He wants me to tell you that each of you have passions, and that you have talents that will help fuel your passion, and that with all of your heart and with all of your soul, you should find a way to use those talents. He wants you to use your gift of love to help others. Finally, he wants me to tell you Neil," she stopped and turned to look at him. She gently touched the cheek of his face, and spoke. "He wants me to tell you that one day, you will make a decision, a very important decision, and that He cannot make this decision for you. You must use what you have learned, draw from the love that fills you, and make the right decision. He…He believes in you, Neil. He loves you. He loves you both so much, and so do I." She let her hand drop from his face, and gently placed the cross in his hand.

"Granny, I don't understand," young Neil said.

The older Neil heard his grandmother's voice for the final time, as he sensed that she was ready to leave on her own terms, and that God and his grandmother Eve were waiting for her.

"You will understand one day, son. You will revisit this day, and you will understand. I love you so much," she said, softly closing her eyes. "I am ready," she whispered as the soul of a wonderful woman left her earthly body and began her final journey home.

Young Neil felt the lump in his throat and chills cross his skin like a breeze. He reached out for Claire's hand and that of his grandmother. Claire's was warm and wet from wiping tears and Granny's was already cool to the touch. He leaned over and kissed her cheek, whispering gently in her ear, "I love you, too."

He then kissed Claire and for the first time realized that he was holding the cross, as one of her tears struck the copper surface. He looked at the inscription once more.

Follow Me

Coming down from the experience was no easy task. In his mind he could still feel a warmness from Granny Lil's soul. When he initially "came back" from the experience, he kept his eyes closed, not wanting to open them and loose the sensation. He knew he was back with the Old Man, he was safe, and the Old Man would respect his privacy by not talking to him right away. In his mind's eye, he saw Granny Lil walk into the loving arms of his other grandmother, Granny Eve.

Had that really happened? He opened his eyes.

Unlike other times, the Old Man was ready to go, and did not seem to want to discuss Neil's experience. Without so much as a grunt, he started walking, just expecting Neil to follow; which he did. Within a few minutes, the Old Man had moved them completely away from the sounds of the river, so that the only noise they heard was the noise they made. One of the noises was rhythmic and not natural. *What is that?*

He could hear the steady thump of the walking stick playing harmony to the rhythmic breathing of the man, but it was the intermittent jingle of something in his cargo pants pocket that always tickled the sound waves of Neil's consciousness...a memory from the past.

Jingle...Thump...Breath...Jingle.

Like the smell of baked bread reminds you of Grandma's house as a kid, there was something about the sound; it was triggering something in him. He thought he had heard it when they first started walking together, after the wreck. *I haven't thought about that in a while...*

Thump...Breath...Jingle.

"What is that?" Neil finally said, pulling himself up to a stop and leaning on a large tree. He looked at the bark and noticed that the moss was in line with the direction in which he was walking: north, he assumed.

Thump...Breath...Smile.

The Old Man stopped, allowing himself to set the hook on what he wanted Neil to see. "What is what?"

"That...well, I don't hear it now, but I have heard it the entire time I have been here. Especially the last few minutes."

"Been here?"

"Yea, the whole time I have been here, with you, walking on this never-ending trail."

The Old Man nodded and smiled; the pupil had taken the teacher's bait and might have swallowed the hook. "Son, this is a path, not a trail. A trail is something that is crafted for everyone to walk on, this path is something that only you will walk on."

Neil closed his eyes and nodded that he had indeed not seen the difference. "Fine, it's a path. I am the only one to walk it. But what is that noise, that *jingle* that I keep hearing?"

The old man pursed his lips together as if he was at the end of the joke. "Does it sound something like this?" He pointed up to the blue sky.

Neil followed his arm to the empty blueness of the sky and saw a seagull fly overhead.

< >

"Look what I found Daddy." Neil looked down from the seagull to find himself on a white sand beach, a familiar place of his youth. A young boy was running toward him with both of his hands out in front of him; white sand and water dripped from his hands as he ran.

"What is it Josh?"

His son was in full little kid sprint, his feet exploding the water of the small tidal pool trying to get to his father with a treasure. As he got closer, the water and sand flowed from the makeshift bowl of his hands, and the compacted prize that he had once held gave way to the forces of dry air and the pounding of five-year-old wind sprints. All Neil heard, as the boy approached, was the jingle of empty shells in his hand.

"Look Daddy," the boy said, skidding to a halt in front of his father, and opening his hands.

Neil stuck his fingers into the cupped hands to move the remaining sand around and reveal the separated halves of two perfect shells. "Those are beautiful, Josh."

The young boy lost the grin of pride on his face and looked down at his hands. In the cupped confines of youthful skin he saw sand, and the perfect structures of two seashells. He started to cry.

Neil looked up from his son's hands to his face and saw the tears gathering. "What wrong buddy?"

"It was one, Daddy."

Neil took the shells from his son's hands and gently put them back together. "You mean like this?"

The young boy nodded.

"Well, when my grandfather was alive, he showed me some very important and neat things about seashells that have come apart."

The boy sniffed, while glancing at his mother, who was standing behind his dad; her stomach was getting big with his little sister. She was smiling and nodding at him.

Neil took one of the two shells and scooped some sand with it. "He taught me that seashells are some of the most useful things that God ever created."

"How?" the boy asked.

"Well," Neil handed the shell back to his son and guided him to scoop the sand, too. "A seashell can be a very valuable tool; see, you can dig with it," and he put his hand on his son's hand and they dug a hole that was deep enough so that the water seeped in. "He said that the seashell is a symbol of determination, fortitude, and hope, and that God always wanted us to have tools like this to work with."

"That's cool" Josh said, sniffing back an earlier tear.

"It is cool, and you know what else he said?"

"What?"

"He said that God made oceans and seashells all over the world so that we could fill our souls and drink from its beauty." Neil scooped the water with the seashell, and showed how it could be a cup to his young son. "Finally, my grandfather said that there is no better beauty on the beach than the single seashell; that is, except for two seashells."

"Why?"

"Well, people seek the beauty of a seashell all over the world. Every day, people will walk beaches everywhere looking for seashells and when they do this, when they seek the prize on the beach among the sand and broken shells, they are seeking God. He was a big believer in God."

"Here," Claire said, handing Neil a string pulled from their kite; she knew what was coming next.

"Thanks hun. And he also said that a child can tie a string around a seashell and craft their first necklace…and that a seashell necklace was actually a loop of grace given by God."

Neil looked over his shoulder and caught a glimpse of his wife, who raised an eyebrow at her husband.

"Wow!" Josh said, amazed at the wonder of his new prize in the only way a child can be in wonder.

Neil felt the encouraging hand of his wife on his shoulder as he threaded both shells together through their holes and tied the square knot of the new necklace around the neck of his son.

Josh turned around proudly to display his prize. The shells jingled as he bounced with joy.

"That's beautiful Josh!" Claire said, beaming at her son.

"You know," the boy said, looking at both of his parents, with a wisdom that was beyond his years, "I will always keep these, they will remind me of the beach, God, and you."

Neil felt the pressure of his wife's hand squeeze his shoulder. She bent down and kissed her boys.

But Josh looked like he had more to say after receiving the sandy kiss on the cheek.

"Mom, do you have more string?"

"I think so dear, let me look."

Josh took the necklace off his neck, thumbing the shells in his hands, never meeting the look of his father.

"Here you go dear," Claire said, passing him the second string.

Josh turned his back on his parents and retreated a few feet so they could not see what he was doing. Claire and Neil looked at each other with knowing smiles.

"If it is that important that God made these to share His grace, and since there are already two, I thought that I should give them each to you," the boy said, handing a separate seashell necklace to each of his parents.

< >

"I had that in the top drawer of my dresser for years. I think I lost it in the last move."

"You did lose it in the last move, son. So did Claire. Josh never knew you lost them, but he asked me in his prayers from time to time if I was sharing my grace with you two since you had the seashells."

"I…I had no idea," Neil said, amazed at the deep belief of his son.

The Old Man took a few steps toward Neil.

Jingle…Jingle.

Neil looked at the Old Man, narrowing his eyes with skepticism as he watched him reach into his pocket. Neil felt the catch in his throat as the man pulled his hand out of his pocket and slowly rolled out his fingers, revealing one of the two halves of the clamshell necklace.

"I thought you might want this back," the Old Man said, handing the seashell to him.

Neil received the shell with gentleness, as if he were being handed a small bird. He accepted the gift in much the same manner his son had all those years ago.

"I am afraid I do not have the other half," the Old Man said with dry affect.

Neil looked from his hand to the Old Man through watery eyes, and then back to the shell. "That's okay."

"I know what you said, the words of your grandfather, they were real…and they are true; they were whispered into the ear of his father many years earlier on a very similar beach," the Old Man said with a wink and he turned around to walk some more.

Neil looked at the simple shell and threadbare string. Nothing meant more to him than this simple gift from his son. He tied the string around his neck, ready to follow the Old Man onto the next part of the path.

Chapter 11

"We've talked a great deal about love, passion, and life, but I want to take some time, while we are on this path to talk about talking."

Neil sensed that this was uncharacteristic of the Old Man and tried to think ahead, about where he was going with this; he was unsuccessful. "We are talking."

"Yes, yes we are. But I am not referring to now, but rather, in your life. Think back. Is our communication ritual, robotic? Is it with passion? Is it only when you are in need?"

"I…I…yea, I think I…I don't know." He gave up.

"Your daughter for instance."

Neil felt a hot flash of intensity pass through his body, causing chilly bumps and the hair on his arms to stand up. He stopped. The Old Man turned around.

"What? Is she…is she okay?"

"Son, she is fine, I am simply trying to make a point."

Neil relaxed.

"Your daughter, and in fact, most children, freely talk with me like I am standing right next to them. And in fact, I am."

"Like they have no barriers."

"Exactly. There is power in their prayers."

< >

Neil had not really wanted to go. He had major deadlines with work; a sales funnel that was never full enough for the bigwig executives, and a supplier issue that was causing his operations people quality problems. When he had signed up for the field trip, he had thought it would be a good time to bond with his daughter.

Claire had approached him early in the school year, knowing how his calendar fills up several months in advance. She sold it well. But, she really didn't have to; Neil knew that his second child had not received half of the attention he had given Josh.

Kathryn was a baby that they thought would never happen. After a routine exam, Claire's doctor had found that one of her fallopian tubes, that they thought were cauterized after Josh was born, had actually reattached. So, Claire had come back from the exam with a little gleam in her eye and a new plan in her heart.

They both decided not to do any medical intervention, if it was meant for them to get pregnant, then so be it. So, this new family position resulted in them ignoring this decision, and the pair having sex all of the time—when the moon was full, when a certain book said so, when they ate shrimp, or drank too much wine. Life revolved around Neil's job, Claire's care for Josh, the upkeep of the house, and the attempts to have the next child. It made for great locker room talk with the guys, but in reality, the pressure to have the second baby, and the picture-perfect family, was intense.

A couple of months into it, Claire was the first to break. She was a stay-at-home mom now, deciding that Josh, a premature baby with emerging special needs, required her more than the nonprofit she had worked for. For the first few years, their schedule revolved around physical and occupational therapies for Josh, staying ahead of the diapers...and the bills. For her, the timing was right for a second child; it was just taking too long. For Neil, the timing was always right, but he was wearing thin.

Tonight had been a typical night since they had decided to go for it full bore: too mechanical and devoid of passion. They had been going at it for almost seven months, and the emotion had drained from the experience. On this particular night, after the deed was done, Claire drew a bath and lowered herself into the hot water, which was laced with the silkiness of bath-store oil. Warm scents of lavender wafted about the room with every swoosh of the water.

Neil produced two glasses of Merlot and sat at the base of the tub, letting the soothing scent roll over him and fill his lungs. They sat quietly for a while, both contemplating what the other one knew they each wanted.

The ritual of the bath had been done hundreds of times; the tub, the wine, and the conversation were something that just happened; it was what they always did, regardless of how robotic the passion had been; the time together helped ground their relationship. Neil enjoyed these moments with his wife; these were the moments where they could reconnect outside of the chaos of life. To Neil, these moments were the raw moments, they were real, anything could be said, as if the warm water and the faux marble tub acted like a peer group where no one judges...they just listen.

Claire enjoyed the rejuvenation of the oily water. She too treasured the time to talk, to really talk to her husband without phone calls, schedules, interruptions, or a little one demanding time between them. But for Claire, tonight's time in the bath was different, this time, when surrounded by waves of steamy lavender, she looked up at her husband and tears pushed past their bounds, trickling down her face and plopping gently into the waves of torment. She didn't fight to control them, and the bath absorbed her pain.

"What's wrong?" Neil asked into his wine glass as his eyes peered over the rim to catch the sight of the tears running down her cheek. She didn't respond at first, but instead swooshed the warm water higher on her body, leaving a silky sheen on her tan skin. "What is it?" Neil asked, perching himself up on his knees getting close to her to ask again.

"I can't do it," she whispered. "I love you so much, but I can't do it anymore Neil."

"You can't do what? Oh," the gravity of her simple confession registered, and he answered his own question. He reached up to stroke her hair and she nuzzled into his hand. "We don't have to you know."

"I know we don't, but, we both want another one."

"Hey, I am great with our family of three," Neil confided the truth. Sex was great...to a point, and they had just reached it.

"Really?"

"Really," he said, holding her head with one hand and stroking her hair with his other.

"I have been doing a lot of praying about this," she said, sniffling. "I am ready to turn it over to God."

He let the confession hang without true response. He had been praying as well, but he was not sure if their prayers matched up. They sat quietly listening to the voices in their souls. They had been here before, and Neil knew how to respond.

"If it is meant to be, then it will be," Neil finally responded, full of inspired resolve that he didn't know he had. "If the Lord wants us to have more, then it will happen. Just like last time. I'm amazed we let it go this far without remembering." He breathed in the scented air deeply. "I am good. We have Josh, and he is a miracle; we should be grateful."

"Yea," Claire nodded, feeling empowered as well, and she reached up and nuzzled his hand, placing gentle kisses along his palm. She looked up at him and smiled, and then kissed his wrist and then the soft skin inside of his elbow, the release of pressure was better than any bath.

Neil drank in the beauty of his wife's blue eyes. Eyes that he had looked into on a cool night when they were kids in a hammock; eyes that he had looked into at the crest of a waterfall when he proposed to her, and eyes that he now looked into, deep with love...and passion. Neil kissed his wife in a way that they had not kissed in seven months. There were no robotic motions, there was no constraint, there was no pressure; there was only love.

Ten years later, Neil found himself wishing to be any other place than on a field trip at the downtown library with his daughter's fourth-grade class. The field trip was an all day event, with the library being the last of three stops in the historic downtown district.

The building facade, a true architectural wonder, displayed the exuberant passions of a society that had too much of everything from the 1920s. A true landmark in the city, the building greeted visitors to its confines with vibrant tile from Italy, marble statues from Greece, and swooping arches that would make Renaissance artisans jealous. Neil noted that with all of the splendor that the building portrayed, it was in stark contrast to the community of homeless that used the building as the back wall of their makeshift homes.

To the homeless of the city, the library was a safe place from the rain, or the cold, or the heat, or if they simply wanted to sit in a comfortable seat. The library, like most libraries in most cities, tolerated these more permanent residents, allowing them to use the services, but not abuse the privilege.

As the flock of school children processed along the main street and through the front door of the classic library, Neil noted that there were several parents in the group that went beyond the call of duty to steer their children clear of any of the riffraff and vagrants. The mother of a tall redheaded girl, a lady that Claire had warned Neil to stay away from, brushed back a swath of fake strawberry-blond hair and asked why "they" were allowed in the library, a question that shocked the socks off of the young librarian who had pulled tour duty for the daily school crowd.

At twenty-two or twenty-three years of age, the small dark-headed librarian, full of helpful intent and ideals from college, nodded as she listened to the question before formulating a response. "As long as people are using the library for what it is intended for, then anyone from our community has the right to be in here," she said, happy that her response was sure to quell any further uncomfortable interrogations. She turned to guide the group to another region. "Ah, here we go," she said moving past early

Egyptian artifacts and into the massive atrium of the library's crown jewel—the children's section.

Neil felt the little fingers in his hand shrink and tug in an attempt to run freely into the child-friendly room that invited the use of all things to do with children's imaginations.

"Are the homeless people allowed in here also?" the strawberry-blond mom asked, not daring to release her child into the room without further assurance.

Neil saw the young librarian turn slowly to address the question; he could almost see her drawing on every master's level course concerning the treatment of uncivilized patrons and counting to ten in her head in an attempt to swallow the answer she really wanted to give.

"Yes."

"Well that isn't really safe now is it?" Strawberry-blond cut her off.

"Ma'am, if you will let me finish."

Strawberry-blond straightened up a bit and nodded.

"Yes, they are allowed, but only if they are with children. We do not let adults alone into this area without accompanying a child." Feeling that she needed to go further, she added. "The area is under camera surveillance as well. We know who goes in and who goes out. Now, for the rest of the parents," she said turning, a beautiful smile magically crossing her face. "Please allow your children to explore. In each corner is a reading house, and in each house, there is a theme."

"What are the themes?" Neil herd the small voice attached to his hand ask.

"Good question," the librarian said, obviously talking to the age group that she was trained for. "What is your name?"

The fourth grader, a blond girl with dark blue eyes looked up at her father for permission to keep talking.

"Go on, it is okay to tell her your name," Neil said.

"My name is Kathryn, but everyone calls me Kat."

"Well Kat," the librarian said, never letting her genuine smile go, "each reading house has a theme, and there are five of them. We have a warrior, knight, and dragon reading house," which was met by a chorus of excitement from the boys in the group. "We have a princess house," which met mixed reviews, "a history house," which met no reaction for the kids, "a science house," which stirred several excited parents to prod their children, "and one we call a Spirit house."

"What's a spirit house?" one of the boys asked.

"Another good question; and what is your name young man?"

"Peter, but don't call me Pete like Kat likes to be...well...Kat," he said, nodding to his classmate.

"Alright then, Peter, we have a collection of artifacts and books about all of the world's beliefs and all of the mythology. The house has pictures and books about ancient Greek mythology and the Roman Gods. It has books about the Buddhist from Asia. It has books in the shape of scrolls that are reproductions from ancient Israel. Finally, it has wonderful pictures of hundreds of churches and the architecture that glorifies God."

"Well, we won't go in that one," Strawberry-blond said under her breath, but loud enough to be heard.

"So, please go explore, and remember we will be in here for thirty minutes before we have to go back to school," the teacher said, moving to talk quietly with the librarian.

Neil looked down at his daughter, she reminded him of a cheetah wanting to pounce. "Go ahead honey, I will be sitting over here checking e-mails," Neil said, pulling his smart phone out of his pocket and thumbing the keys as he walked toward some chairs on the side of the room. Several of the parents took his lead and headed toward the makeshift workstation of tiny wooden chairs and knee-high tables.

< >

"You were lost in your work life and not in the interest of your daughter. You missed the calling of joy," the Old Man said bluntly. He didn't let Neil respond, but instead continued with the lesson. "Joy is simple to find Neil. It is like the beams of a rising sun. You may be looking at the beauty, but are you feeling the warmth of the beauty? A child is as simple, you can look at a child, and go through the motions of raising a child, but if you don't take the opportunity to share the wonder from a child's eyes, and embrace the experience, then you miss the joy. The joy of a child is far warmer than the rays of the sun, but you must allow yourself to move from the shadows to feel it."

Neil nodded, rolled his eyes, and shook his head. "How could I have been so stupid?"

"I don't think stupid is the right word. You should not be hard on yourself. You were doing what you thought was right: not doing what your heart knew was right. Go on though, tell me more."

< >

From the hard comfort of his tiny wooden chair, Neil looked up long enough to see his daughter trace a finger along the clay dome of the Spirit House learning area and then tentatively disappear inside. He knew she would go to that one first. She loved church, and that one seemed to call to her. Comforted in the thought that she was happy, he lowered his head and went back to crisis e-mails from employees that sent e-mails just to send e-mails.

Kat took small tentative steps into the Spirit Learning area. The "house" was really a large portion of the greater room. It was domed with slate-colored roofing tiles that were distressed, making them look like they were plied off of a cathedral in Rome.

The inside of the structure was darker than the outside room and about twice the size of Kat's bedroom at home. The room was divided into sections and display lights illuminated each section of wall. The lights brought life to artifacts, books, paintings, and items that the students could touch, but not take.

Kat quickly counted twelve sections and started moving through them. The first section that caught her eye was an area dedicated to the Indian priests and medicine men of the early North American Indian Tribes. She traced her hand along the feathers and watched the LED lights of the fake fire in the picture of an Indian ritual.

"I think that they're asking for their sick people to be healed," Kat heard a little voice from behind her say. She turned around to see a smaller girl standing in the shadows behind her. Kat didn't recognize her from her class and didn't think that any other class was in the children's area.

"What did you say?"

The smaller girl moved closer, eclipsing the shadows of the dark room and entering the man-made light of the sectional wall. She was about six inches shorter than Kat, but she had similar hair and their eye color was identical.

Kat accepted her without question, only as kids do. "How do you know?"

The smaller girl moved closer to the living painting and touched the old woman who was stretched out on a deer skin next to the pulsing LED fire. "She is the one that is sick. Look. Touch," she said, taking Kat's hand and putting her fingers on the picture. "You can feel her. She's hot."

Kat thought about that for a minute, and before her mind went too far, she just accepted that the Indian woman in the picture was sick because she was warmer than her fingers.

"And him," the younger girl pointed to the man with the full headdress, "he is the chief, and the girl that is sick is his daughter."

Kat looked at the chief, with hundreds of glorious eagle feathers pointing up to the sky. With a hat as beautiful as the one that draped from his tan forehead, he had to be special. He had to be important.

"But here is the most important person," the smaller girl confessed. "He is the medicine man, the healer. He can sing a song, or light a fire, or just get down on his knees and ask God to heal the daughter of the chief."

"So, why doesn't he?" Kat asked with innocence.

The smaller girl didn't answer, but instead moved past Kat to get closer to the painting. She placed her fingers on the medicine man and bowed her head. Kat watched her, tracing her fingers around the medicine man figure. Kat let her eyes drift from the painting and for the first time she took notice of the girl's appearance.

She wore dirty sneakers and socks that did not match. She had on jeans, but they were dirty, as if she had been sitting in fields or on sidewalks. She shrouded herself with a pullover hoodie that was a size too large, and on closer inspection, was threadbare and looked stiff. Kat let her gaze follow up to the back of her head; finally noting her hair, hair that would have normally been beautifully dirty blond, was just dirty and full of tangles. The smaller girl had pulled her hair back into a ponytail using a green rubber band like one that would hold a batch of broccoli from the store.

"Who do you know that's sick?" Kat asked without thinking, she just knew.

The girl turned, her hand still on the medicine man. "My Dad."

"What's wrong with him?"

The smaller girl dropped her hand off of the medicine man and her eyes fell to the floor like shooting stars jumping from Heaven. "He drinks."

Kat thought about that for a minute before responding. Her parents drink alcohol. It was common for them to each have a few glasses of wine after her dad came home from work, but they seemed okay. They weren't sick, and they certainly didn't need a medicine man.

"My parents drink, but they are not sick; my dad is out there, see!" She pointed through the doorway to her father. Neil's head was down as he piloted his fingers through more important issues on his smart phone.

"My dad is different," the smaller girl said, withdrawing slightly from the lighted section, almost wishing she hadn't reached out. The shadow that had hidden her earlier now drew a line across her face, but did little to hide her emotion.

Kat watched the girl take a few steps back, and then remembered what she had learned in Sunday School the weekend before.

"What if we pray for your father? Do you think that would help?" Kat asked, stopping the girl in her tracks, but not before a single tear rolled down the smaller girl's face, crossing from darkness to light.

"Pray for him, my dad, you mean like the medicine man?"

"Well kind of, I guess." Kat struggled to vocalize what she felt. "In our church, in our Sunday School, we learned that there is power in prayer and that sometimes prayers are answered in ways that we will never know."

The smaller girl looked up at the medicine man, the fire, and the chief's daughter lying on the deer skin. "Will you come with me and pray?"

"Oh, well, I kind of thought we could do it…here," Kat said, suddenly feeling uncomfortable, and regretting the suggestion; she glance at her father, who still had his head down.

"It will only take a few minutes. He's right outside," the smaller girl said, taking Kat's hand and pulling her toward the door.

"Alright class, it's time to assemble," Neil heard the teacher say, breaking him from his e-mail trance and allowing him to stand and stretch his legs. He looked around, smiling at all of the fourth-grade children as they filed back into the area. He saw the teacher point a finger in the air, silently counting each pupil. But Neil was faster. He was not counting heads: He was looking for one face in the crowd, one particular person that was just less than four feet with blond hair and blue eyes. He was looking for his daughter.

"Well, I seem to be missing one, "the teacher said, with agitation.

"Yea," Neil said, suddenly feeling the rush of warmth flood the skin of his neck. "I think it's my daughter.

"Where else can they go?" Neil asked with a tone of accusation toward the librarian.

Clearly flustered and lost for words, the librarian looked around the room, taking in each of the five learning centers and then looking back at the parent. "I don't know, if they aren't here," she said.

Neil took off, searching each of the learning centers. He ducked his head into each of the areas, calling her name, not caring if he was disturbing others in the library. "She's not here. What about the cameras, do you have the tape we can look at?" he said, pointing to the cameras on the wall.

The librarian muttered something before straightening herself for an admission. "The cameras are fake, we don't have the budget for real ones. I'm sorry to say that we don't have any video of where your daughter is," she said, feeling sick to her stomach. She then moved off to call the supervisor and within seconds, an audible alarm was blaring, a verbal "Code Adam," signaling the disappearance of a child.

Neil closed his eyes and rubbed his face with his hands to try and center himself. He found himself silently whispering a prayer for his daughter. He could hear automated locks closing on all of the doors around him. They were locks that could help or hurt; they were false hope and that was something that he didn't need now. He grabbed his phone and was about to run toward the main lobby when he heard a small voice stop him in his tracks.

"I think I know where she is. Kat. I think I know where she is." Neil spun around, thanking God for the angelic voice that had just spoken to him.

< >

"You know I heard you," the Old Man said, peering deeply at his pupil.

"I had no idea," Neil said, feeling a tinge of shame.

"I know, which is sad, but, I hear all of my children calling to me. I hear them thanking me. I hear them cursing me, arguing with me, talking, wishing, hoping, asking, and even begging; I hear them all," the Old Man added.

"I would never ask without really meaning it."

"Of course you would, don't lie to me, everyone asks for little things without meaning it. But, I know when you really mean it. I know when you have passion, when you believe, when you deny and especially when you forget everything that has been taught to you and you simply surrender yourself to me. I like that one. Neil, don't ever stop talking to me, just because you don't hear me answer, I am still listening…to everything! And, so is your daughter," the Old Man said, letting Neil slide back into his reflection about Kat.

< >

The younger girl was still pulling Kat further away from the Children's section of the library. They had "escaped" through the emergency exit that did not have a working alarm. They emerged on Twenty-first Street , a main throughway in the city. A cool wind filed along the edges of the buildings, whipping up leaves and the odor of the street.

"He's right over here," the smaller girl said, dragging Kat behind her.

Kat let herself be pulled by the tug of the young girl. She knew that what she was doing went against everything her parents had taught her about interacting with strangers, but somewhere deep inside, she also knew that what she was doing was the right thing to do.

"It's right here," the small girl said, leading Kat near the entrance of the library and to the front of one of the large cardboard boxes propped up against the main library wall.

"I can't go in there," Kat said, pulling the duo to a halt.

"Why not?" the smaller girl asked, stopping a few feet from her home.

"Well…well…I don't know," Kat said thinking like the child that she was.

"But you said you could pray, pray like they do in your church, you said that in there," the smaller girl said, her grip on Kat's hand tightening.

Kat thought of all of the lessons he parents had taught her, and being dragged into a cardboard box by a small girl was not one of them. "I can pray, but I don't know if it's it safe…safe…in there," she said slowly, with a nod to the box.

The girl stopped tugging on her savior, stopping feet from the box opening. "It's my dad. He's not perfect, he drinks every day, and when he's not drinking he's looking for money to buy something to drink. Sometimes I have to find it for him. He doesn't look for money for us to eat, or for shoes, or for anything. But, even though we live in a box, I know it's the best that he can do, and I know he cares…he cares for me. And, I want to help him so he can care for both of us." She looked up into the taller girl's eyes, a girl who wore fashionable shoes and smelled pretty. She looked at a girl, which under different circumstances, could pass for her older sister. "Of course it's safe, it's just my father. Can you help us?"

Without a verbal answer, Kat swallowed hard and with the smaller girl's hand still in hers, she ducked her head into the box that was propped up on the outside wall of the library.

"Pete," Neil said, turning quickly to bend down in front of the boy who his wife had told him had a "thing" for Kat.

"Peter, it's Peter, not Pete," Peter said, oblivious to the importance of the information that he held.

Neil closed his eyes quickly in reprimand of himself for not remembering that simple detail.

"Peter, stop playing, tell him where Kat is," the teacher said, also crouching down beside the student.

"Well, she, well I kind of, well," he muttered, feeling the sudden pressure of the adults upon him.

"Son," Neil said, reining in all of his angst and trying to channel the calm that he knew would be the only thing that would help him retrieve the information necessary to find his daughter. He put himself in "sales" mode, something that he often did with his customers. They were the most important people to Neil when he was in front of them, and he wanted them to know it, just like he now wanted Peter to know it. "You are not in any trouble, in fact, you're a hero."

Peter looked at the man and then at his teacher and then at the librarian, and they were all nodding, but the librarian was wiping tears from her face. "A Hero, why am I a hero?"

"Because you are brave and bold. You know something that is going to help us find Kat, don't you?" The boy nodded with assurance. "Do you want to show me instead of telling me; in fact, you can help me find her; kind of like going on a secret mission."

The teacher, catching onto the parent's line of psychology, jumped right in. "Can you take the class to a very secure location and wait for us to return," she said to the librarian, who was already jumping into motion.

"Alright class and parents, please let's go in here," she said shepherding the class away from the situation.

"All right Peter, can you take us to find Kat?" he asked, taking his hand off of his shoulder as if he was releasing a tracking dog to find a prize. Peter moved off to the other side of one of the learning centers with the two adults in tow. He stopped at a large grate in the wall that had hinges.

"They wanted me to close it behind them and stay here, but I followed them instead," the boy said, still feeling that this was more like being in trouble than a secret mission.

"Who was it that took Kat?" the teacher asked.

"She wasn't taken, she went on her own," he said, to the shock of both adults. Neil felt his heart hurt that much more. He reached for his phone again, but he wasn't going to make the call that he dreaded until he knew something.

"Show us where they went son," Neil said, opening the grate and watching him step through to a hallway behind the wall. The grate was not attached to anything, Neil noted as he stepped through, but the sight of the exit door propped open made his heart sink.

"Who is this?" a man said in a raspy voice.

Kat tried to let her eyes adjust to the darkness of the enclosure, but the stinging of the air made her blink and rub at her eyes. "Why are my eyes stinging?"

"Daddy, this is Kat, she is a friend and she is going to pray for you," the smaller girl said, ignoring Kat's question about the stinging air.

Kat's eyes slowly adjusted and through the water she blinked away, she could see a lump in the corner of the small shelter. The lump vaguely resembled the shape of a skinny man. He had long unkempt hair and his beard was ragged at best. Kat could see dark rings around his eyes and his skin was yellowish. She felt everything in her body tell her to turn and run out of the box, run away from the stinging air, run away from the smell...

"Kat, please help," the small girl said, pulling her back to the instant of the reality.

"Take my hand, both of you," Kat said, suddenly focused, and believing in the stories of Jesus holding the hands of the sick to be true.

With a look to his daughter, the lump of a man in the corner lifted his hand to the taller pretty girl as he rose to his knees. His hand was bony and cold. His fingernails were dirty and yellow; she squeezed a little harder.

Kat bent her knees to the ground, feeling the concrete piercing through the dark leggings that her mother liked. She looked at both of them, the daughter of a man who lived in a box, and the man of a daughter that let them live this way. She decided that it was not for her to judge them, something that both her mother and father had taught her. She did what she said she would do. She did what she hoped others would do for her if she ever needed it: She began to pray.

"May the Lord be with you," Kat said, not knowing what they would say.

"And also with you," the lump of a man whispered from a place that he had long forgotten about.

Peter pushed the door open and looked up and down the street at the rows of boxes. Each box was not the same as the next, but each box served the same purpose; the protection of a human being. On his heels were his teacher and Kat's dad.

"Well, Peter, where to from here?" Neil asked, looking across the street and down the streets for any sign of a girl. It was cold and there were not many people out. It was at that moment that he realized that she might be in one of the boxes.

"Which one are they in Peter?"

The boy moved left and then right, feeling flustered to remember.

"Down there, that one I think, at the end," the boy said, pointing at one of the larger boxes near the entrance to the library. They had walked right past that one on their way into the building.

"Dear Lord," Kat began. She had never prayed in public, and she had never prayed for someone. Her mom or dad usually said the blessing at dinner, and it had been awhile since she had said prayers before bed, but something inside of her helped her form the words. Something inside of her filled her with confidence; something inside of her let her simply give love; something that her parents told her she would always be able to give others. "We thank you for allowing us all to come together and ask for your forgiveness. I would like to ask that you please wrap your loving arms around…around," she looked up at the two people she was praying for. "What are your names?"

"This is Brittany and I am Don," the skinny man, Don, said, giving life to himself.

Kat closed her eyes again. "Like I was saying, please dear Lord, wrap your loving arms around Don and Brittany. They need your help. They need your forgiveness and like the medicine man does, they need to be healed. All of this I ask in your name. Amen."

Neil threw the flap of the box open with such aggression that the entire flap ripped off, causing one of the walls to collapse outward and letting light flood the scene in front of him, and his heart stopped.

Kat, not startled, opened her eyes. She was still holding the hands of the homeless father and daughter, as they all kneeled in prayer. "Daddy," she said standing before her father could grab her in a bear hug that he was never going to let go of.

"Oh thank God, oh thank God," he kept saying, before his eyes opened and he looked at the homeless man and his daughter. In the flash of an instant, Neil knew that he was going to kill the man that held his daughter in a box, until he recognized the face of the man staring back at him.

< >

"Why do you let people get like that?" Neil asked with sincere question and with no accusation.

"I do not let my children get like that. You have free will son. You make decisions, and you live by those decisions. Would you prefer that Man be at the end of strings like puppets?" the Old Man said, having had this discussion many, many times.

"But he had so much." Neil had met the man from the box several times in the past; he used to work for one of Neil's customers in town.

"Neil, have you forgotten that when your daughter courageously cried out to me to help, that I *did* answer her prayers, and I *did* help. Son, I sent you."

Neil nodded, accepting that he had been a tool of grace, and like so many times before, he had been unaware.

"After that day, Claire and I worked with their church to help Don get the treatment he needed," Neil kept talking, knowing full well that the Old Man knew how this story ended. "It was great. Brittany stayed at our house." Neil smiled to himself allowing the happy thoughts to fill him. "Kat was the perfect big sister for her. They're still friends," his voice trailed off as another thought, the thought that underlined this entire memory, begged to be asked. The Old Man pushed him for the question.

"What is on your mind, son?"

"Well, when we talk, when we pray, when we cry out to God, you say that you answer." Neil said the words carefully; he wanted to get this right. He wanted to understand and he wanted to be able to explain this later.

"Go ahead," the Old Man said, rocking back and forth on his walking stick like a tall blade of wheat in a golden field.

"You answer us…you speak to us, right?"

"I answer you, yes. I speak to you, yes. But," he held an elderly finger up to stop Neil before he could follow up with another question, "you do not always hear what it is that I have to say." He let that sink in, allowing the pause to permeate into Neil's soul.

"Because we want to hear what we want you to say."

"Yes."

"And you don't always speak to us the way we think you should," Neil confirmed.

"Yes."

"Are you saying that we should stop trying to listen?"

"No, son, I am saying that I want you to be open to what I am saying, and *how* I am saying it. Neil, I can speak to you in more ways than there are grains of sand on all of the beaches of the world. I can put the whisper of comfort in the breeze of a summer day, or fill your heart with the passion of a songbird's call, or I can put people in your path that serve my purpose. Like with Kat and Brittany," he said raising an eyebrow. "Most new associations are because I want you to experience something from that person. Neil, I talk to you all of the time, through scripture, through song, through visions, through feelings, through thought, and directly, as we are talking now. There is nothing that I enjoy more than to have a conversation with my children. You just need to be open and listen to how we are communicating."

"You have said several times that along our path that you are listening," Neil stated.

"I am."

"I believe you now."

CHAPTER 12

They had descended back down to the valley. The Old Man mentioned something about seeing the end of the river, so that is the way they were headed. As with before, the sound of the river preceded the sight of the water. The sound rose up and met Neil as he walked, absorbing his thoughts. The majestic river that they had been following in one way or another rumbled by in front of them, oblivious to their quest, only intent on moving forward. Every so often, the surface of the river would smooth over, offering faux tranquility; but Neil knew better. In these areas of smoothness, an unexpected burst of bubbles or swirl usually signaling the presence of the current that churned below. He was glad the Old Man had brought them back down to the water; under current torments or not.

Neil found his thoughts wandering above the currents; his eyes finding a stick or leaf that bobbed along the flow in a final river ride. He looked over at the Old Man every once in awhile. He had been quiet for the better part of an hour as they both rested by the river. This was the longest amount of time that they had spent sitting still. Neil needed the rest. He was tired, and he was thankful for the time; so his mind went back to the river.

Very aware of Neil's lucid thoughts, the Old Man was content with letting this string of moments be. This was a time of reflection, he had designed this in for the purpose that it was intended; he wanted Neil to reflect on what had been given to him.

Neil thought about the water, this water, and in one way or another for most of their journey they had been following it. It had started with no more than fog settling on leaves high in the mountains, in turn dripping into puddles, and then, through the course of the natural flow, grew into a creek, and then a stream, and then a small river, and now…and now, it was a beautiful river, brimming with life and raw splendor. It was in this splendor that Neil let his mind wander and his body relax. He tried to empty his mind of everything except for the experiences he had lived with the Old Man. His soul, something that he felt had turned hard like dried clay, was now slowly being reformed and recast by a master artisan. *But cast into what?*

Each scene from his journey played out in his head. Any one of them could bring him to tears, or to laugh or to shake with apprehension. They were impactful, real, raw, and full of emotion. But like the river that flowed in front of him, there was more to what he was being allowed to see. There was an undercurrent— something that he had not yet grasped was there, something that moved the big boulders and ground the elements into sand. It was not positive, but it was present; like a small voice in your head casting doubt. It was a current, flowing under the fabric of life. It was a current that would manifest itself in rattles of fear, waves of sadness, lead weights of desperation, and even empty joy and mock love. *Have I not faced these down on this path? Am I not riding a river of God's Grace?*

"Do you know what works against me the most?" The Old Man asked, breaking the silence and Neil's self doubt.

Startled, Neil looked over toward him. He was sitting on an old weather-beaten log with his feet outstretched. With determination, he was pushing his walking stick into the dirt trying to work a smaller stick free from Nature's confines.

"No," Neil said with slight wonderment, "what would scare you the most?"

The Old Man smiled. "Ah," he said popping the lone stick out of the sand and fishing it in with his walking stick. "I did not say 'fear,' I said 'works against me.' " He held his stare for a moment. "Interesting that you substituted the word fear for my question about what works against me. Very interesting."

"What? I didn't say that!"

"You did, in so many words, son."

Neil had learned that when the Old Man referred to him as 'son,' he really wanted something he was saying to stick. Neil chewed on the exchange for a moment, thinking that perhaps it was fear that worked against him. *Was fear the current under the calm on the surface?*

"So, why do you think fear works against you?" the Old Man persisted, turning his new smaller stick over in his hand.

"I don't know if the words; 'works against me,' is really accurate. Okay, I admit that I let things like *doubt* work against me, but I am not fearful of it."

"Really?"

Neil let the retort hang as he thought about the answer. He thought through his experiences again. The fear in those seemed tangible; real danger…the fear of getting lost, or of a tornado, or of being killed. It wasn't the same type of fear as what the Old Man was signaling it to be. *Was it?*

"What about the experiences you have *not* relived on our walk? What about the tough choices in your life? The ones that revolve around your innermost passions, your innermost beliefs, your innermost loves? Do you know how to even acknowledge these…let alone know how to deal with them?"

Neil opened his mouth to speak, but he had nothing to say. His mind spun around the questions, more like accusations from the old man. Were they right? Had he ever really acknowledged his passion, his beliefs, his love? Or, had he slowly locked the door on these innermost pillars as the demands of life cast its hooks into him? He had wanted to be a writer when he was a kid. He wanted to help his wife set up a mission in Central America. Why hadn't he done these things?

"Our walks," he ventured slowly with a response, "have been eye-opening to me. I can see that I am not supposed to let these…these *fears*…in my life, that there is no room for such emotions when I have grace filling me up.

The Old Man smiled, raising a proud eyebrow at his pupil. "Good. That is very very good Neil. So you say you have learned to keep these out of your life and just be filled with grace?"

Tentatively, Neil nodded.

"So," the Old Man turned darkly. "Why are you so filled with anger?"

Neil felt the flush of blood warm his face as he fought back the urge to lie to the man and deny the question. *Hadn't they just had a great breakthrough moment? And now this?* Instead Neil lowered his head, stuck his hands in his pockets, and kicked lightly at the dirt on the trail, flinging a pebble into the grass.

The Old Man waited, he knew this game, he had many children, and all children act this way when they want to hide something. So, he waited.

Neil continued to swirl the dirt with his shoe. He was not ready to talk. He wasn't angry. Nothing that they had talked about even came close to talking about anger. The fear thing he got, but not anger. Why would the old guy ask such a question?

"I…I don't know what you mean," he said, surprising himself with the vocal answer.

The Old Man nodded, accepting that at least the child had answered. "Is that a truthful answer? Is that the answer you really want to tell me...and yourself?"

"Why is it even important?" Neil didn't like how this line of questioning had turned on a dime against him.

The Old Man played his card, a card that he had held the entire time. "Well, son, I believe that one of the main reasons you are here, here with me, is because of the anger that burns inside of you."

"Really?" Neil asked defiantly.

"Really, and I want you to come to grips with it before you do something for me."

"I am not angry, I tell you," Neil repeated his earlier claim, trying to drive a stake into his position. He could give a rip about doing something for the Old Man. Especially since he had called him out on some mystical anger that he supposedly carried around with him. *That is pure crap.*

"Really?" the old man said, raising an eyebrow at the younger man's obstinate thoughts. So much like a child. Hence the reason that he always waited so long into a journey like this to broach the subject.

"Why do *you* think I am angry?"

And there it was, the breakthrough that the Old Man wanted. He thought about that for a few seconds before responding. "Well, I could tell you that every time a butterfly flaps its wings to rise into the air I know about it. I could tell you that I hear the symphonic crash of every wave that curls onto a beach, and finally I could tell you that every prayer, every word spoken, every emotion felt by my children I also hear and feel." The old man took a step toward Neil so that the blue of his eyes washed over the younger man like a lighthouse beacon to a lost ship. "I can tell you all of these wonderful things, but I don't have to: son, you told me."

Neil knew it to be true. He knew that at the very core of everything—the failure of his company, the slipping relationship with his kids and Claire—his entire disconnect was because he had started down a path of anger, and it was an easy path to stay on. Why choose to be happy when it seemed like everything was not. The trip to the mountains was supposed to fix all that had recently divided the family, but even that had been peppered with fighting and anger.

"Son, I know why you are angry, and I know why you shelter yourself in fear, and it isn't your job, or your kids or Claire. I want you to know that I am here for you."

"Alright I give. I won't pretend to hold back or even pretend to know what you are talking about."

"Is it that easy for you?"

"What?"

"The deception, your own deception, how you lie to yourself; and to me?"

Neil stood silent, trying to not think of anything; he wanted to keep his mind blank, unreadable. He wanted to keep his anger down. He was guarding his feelings, hiding his thoughts and denying his opportunity to make amends.

The Old Man had had this conversation hundreds of thousands of times and in hundreds of thousands of locations. In most situations where he would ask his children a question, he would wait them out for an answer, but this subject, unlike any subject that he ever broached with humanity, needed something more. It needed action. It needed a strong hand. It needed hard questions and harder reality. Most people did not openly admit that they feed off fear and anger.

"Why are you so angry?" he simply asked again.

This time, the question ignited the air, a burning acquisition, it reverberated like thunder on the cliffs of mountains; it pierced something inside of Neil. The question pulled at something, trying to shake it free, something he could not put his finger on. It was deep and personal and it had been hidden in a dark place. This place, a region that he never shared, never acknowledged, a place that was seldom visited, like a distant relative in a prison: This dark place had never been cracked, let alone, explored. He rarely shared this place with his wife, let alone himself, let along God.

The Old Man knew what to do next, and uncharacteristic to the entire walk that they had been on, he told Neil what to expect. "I need you to get to the bottom of this anger. I want you to meet some people that I know; it will allow you to let me help you," he simply said.

Skeptical and still trying to keep his mind blank, Neil nodded, not really wanting to go any further than were they were right now. This place of anger was not supposed to be seen, let alone visited. It was locked away for a reason, and letting it out would cause hurt, pain, and sorrow.

With a simple nod from the Old Man, the shadows started to disappear. The temperature began to drop and a cool mist started rolling in through the trees. Like a mountain slicing through a river of clouds the mist rolled in thicker and thicker. The Old Man disappeared in the fog, and Neil lost reference. He began to shiver. Dampness pushed on all parts of his exposed skin.

"Where are you?" he called out, trying to find the Old Man in the mist.

"I am here."

"Where?" Neil was disoriented. He spun around, seeking the direction of the voice.

"I am here, as always, with you."

Neil was sweating again, but it was not from the heat. His breathing turned to gulps of air and his senses verged on panic. He found himself more and more disoriented in the fog; and tentatively shuffled his feet forward, his arm outstretched in an attempt to find anything to hold on to. The first scream that pierced the fog shook Neil to the core.

"What are you making me do?" Neil cried out. There was another scream in the fog. A man was in pain somewhere beyond Neil's vision.

"I am not making you do anything that you do not want to do on your own," the Old Man's voice spoke through the fog.

"Why are they screaming?" Neil could hear others—people—somewhere in the mist. They screamed out in pain.

"Why are you angry? I am here."

"I'm not! Where?"

"You only need to call my name and I am here when you need me."

"I don't know what to do?"

"You only need to call my name and I am here when you need me."

"But I am scared."

"Then we are starting to get somewhere."

< >

Neil stopped stumbling, freezing in place, when he felt a hand grab his arm."

"What'cha you doing here, man? Get down!"

Neil obeyed the voice behind the hand that held his arm. He crouched low. There was suddenly a putrid acidic smell in the air. He could smell dirt, more like mud, mixed with an acid plantlike smell, and something like gunpowder. He felt like puking right there.

"Look Mac, you're gonna get killed doing shit like that!"

Shit like what? "Sorry," he heard an unfamiliar voice come out of his mouth.

"Well, you better learn quick man, or you go home in a black bag. Got it?"

Neil shook the fog from his head and as he did, the misty foul-smelling fog around him began to dissipate and lift as well. "Got it," he said slowly as he watched the sun burn through the fog on a plane of hell he never thought he would ever experience.

"You okay man? You look all pale and all ghostly."

Neil looked at the man who still held his arm. He knew the face. "Yea…yea, I'm okay. Where are we?"

The other man let Neil's arm go and reached for something in a small pouch slung across his shoulder. "What'cha talking about, man?"

"Where are we?" Neil repeated the question; and then he saw the last name of the man. It was stitched across his left chest pocket…it was Neil's last name. Abrams.

"Oh man," Abrams said, producing a hand grenade from his pocket and pulling the pin with his teeth. "We are in Nam man," he said, spitting the pin and throwing the grenade over the foxhole wall. "Cover me newbie," he said jumping over the wall and firing his M-16.

Neil watched the man leap over the wall, bathed in the flashing light of his rifle firing round after round. And it was at that moment that he realized that he was also holding his own M-16.

"*Get in the fight Mac!*" a man yelled, jumping over the foxhole and following after Abrams.

Neil looked down at his clothing; he was wearing a uniform, a green uniform; the same one he knew his father had worn in Vietnam. On his chest, across his left pocket was the name MacMillan.

"*Why have you done this to me?*" Neil cried out, throwing the rifle to the ground and leaning his head against the foxhole. *You only asked why I am angry, not why I hate my father.* He never heard another person crawl into the hole beside him.

"Hey brother, you okay? You'd better move. Com'on!" Neil felt the hand on his shoulder; a warm touch was tugging at him to move. His feet felt like cinder blocks cast in the jungle mud. He didn't want to go anywhere and anger bubbled to his surface.

"Get off!" Neil shook his arm free.

"We's gotts to go…now!" the man said, grabbing Neil's arm again and pulling at his platoon brother to move from the hole.

Neil looked over at the man, really a kid, maybe nineteen years old. He had mud mixed with stubble across his face, a pack of cigarettes strapped to his helmet and he was as skinny as a fire pole. But in his eyes, his brown eyes, he could see something that looked vaguely familiar.

"What are you, hard of hearing or something?" the skinny kid demanded. "The L-T's called in a strike, we's gotts to go!" He was no longer warm and inviting. "*Pick that damn thing up and let's go!*"

Neil grabbed the rifle and let the skinny kid pull him from the hole. At that moment, as he breached the top of the wall, the sounds of war engulfed his soul. The percussions of exploding ordinance in the field in front of them were deafening. Each explosion seemed to suck the air away from around them with every new crater created. There was also a constant wiz of lead flying through the air like swarms of angry hornets looking for the guy that just knocked down the nest.

Neil moved his body into a run, following the other man, and as he did, he slowly started to accept where he was. But he had no idea why he was here. *If the Old Man thought I was angry before!* He looked at the beanpole kid soldier that had pulled him from the hole just as two jets screamed overhead.

"*Hit the dirt man!*" Beanpole yelled, grabbing Neil's arm and flinging him down into a rice field.

The concussion was tremendous, and it vibrated every organ in their bodies, but it was the heat, the overwhelming heat, that washed over them, sucking all of the moisture from his skin like bacon in a microwave. Neil kept his head down as the wave of fire worked its magic against the enemy. He held his breath for as long as he could; knowing that the slightest intake of air would scar his lungs. He cracked one of his eyes open to see what was happening around him. In the reflection of the rice water he saw his shadow engulfed in a thunderstorm of orange. *He has sent me to Hell.*

"Alright Man, I think it's good to go," Beanpole said an instant later, slapping Neil on the back. Neil lifted his head to a version of anguish that no man should ever experience. *Dante had no idea about this level, or this type of inferno!*

Neil shook the concussion of the ordinance and heat from his head, slowly letting his senses come back to him. His ears were ringing and there was a new smell in the air. The sounds of war had given way to the crackling of a giant bonfire of the likes he had never seen. Liquid fire stuck to everything, and trees coursing with sap and oil sent up a plume of black smoke. Seared death smelled terrible, but the screams had stopped.

"The Lord your God is with you, He is mighty to save," Beanpole said as he slapped Neil's shoulder and walked toward his gathering platoon of brothers.

"You have no idea."

"What did you say?"

"What have you done with me Old Man?" Neil said quietly, falling in line behind Beanpole.

Neil reached into his head, closing his eyes as he walked. He fully expected to be transported back to the riverside and the Old Man. He was already trying to dissect just what he had been through on this experience and what exactly it meant to his greater character, the path he was supposed to be walking and his meaning in life…and all the rest of the yadda, yadda…

"Hey, watch it!"

Neil opened his eyes abruptly to see that he had not been transported back to the river, but had instead run into the back of Beanpole.

"Ahh…sorry," Neil looked around confused: no river, no Old Man, just death, heat, and a small group of men that wished to be anywhere but here. He was just like them.

What are you doing with me? Neil dealt the question to the Old Man in his mind. There was no answer. *I thought you said you were with me? That you would answer me?*

"Alright, who are we missing?" Abrams said. He was the first guy that had been in the foxhole with Neil and had just reappeared from the direction that had just been scorched.

A sergeant visually counted each soldier's helmet before sounding off. "Looks like one L-T."

"One! Shit! Is that it? I thought half you newbies would be toast after that fight. Who is it Sarge?" the lieutenant asked.

"Ahhh" the sergeant said, looking at each face now.

"It's Shelby Sarge," one of the other men said with little emotion.

"Who was with Shelby?" the sergeant asked with an equal amount of compassion.

Neil watched each man hold his head down in solitude, not wanting to admit that they were with the new guy as he met death.

"I saw him take off after you L-T," Beanpole spoke up. "He was on his own. It was right before the 'palm hit, sir."

"Shit," Lt. Abrams said, shaking his head at the action. "Okay, Ricks and you," he said pointing to Beanpole and Neil. "What's your name?"

Neil felt the faces of the other soldiers upon him as the lieutenant called him out. He looked down at his uniform.

"Mac…MacMillan…sir." He knew that name, too.

"Mac, right. Okay, you and Ricks, since you saw him last, get in there and see if you can find what's left of Shelby."

Neil watched Beanpole/Ricks snap off a quick, "Yes sir," and then take off for the burning remains of the jungle.

Neil held his gaze on the lieutenant before moving out. For the first time, things started to click. He felt his insides turn upside down and he started after Ricks at a run, getting away from the other men, before anyone saw him puke. The man that had just ordered him into the pit of Hell was a man that he recognized…the man was his father.

< >

"Are you kidding me?" Neil could sense that he was back along the river. He was bent over as if he was still in the action of getting sick. In the blink of an eye, he had returned. But he still felt like puking.

"I asked you a simple question, you know?" the Old Man stated.

Neil took a deep breath, the smoke had gone, and the clean air settled his lungs…although the smell of death still lingered in his nose. The shock of the movement between one phase and another was lost on him this time. A number of emotions churned inside of his soul like a cement mixer.

"What the hell did you do?" Neil asked in a whisper. His head was still down. He did not want to look at the Old Man. He was truly angry now.

"I asked you a question."

"You sent me to Hell." Neil stood up and faced the Old Man.

"I asked you a question. Is Hell where you have to go to get the answer?"

Neil looked up at the Old Man's eyes, but unlike before he did not want to feel the tendrils of grace. For the first time on their walk, he felt anger toward the man.

"That's alright, it happens," the Old Man sensed the anger and brushed it off. "But I still need you to find that answer for me. Right now, you are just wearing a mask that resembles the answer, but it's not the answer that I seek."

Neil stood for several minutes looking past the Old Man to the flowing river, trying to gather his wits about him and determine just what he really felt. He wasn't answering any damn question, especially not after being sent there.

The old man nodded with the wisdom of the universe, walked over to Neil, and placed his hand on his shoulder. Neil tensed.

"When you are ready, I will be here," the Old Man said, sending him back.

< >

Neil found the motion of the zipper of the black canvas bag familiar and alien all at the same time. For so many things, the zip meant warmth, or shelter, but in this case, it symbolized the final ride out of Vietnam for one of his brothers. He pulled the zipper closed and patted the side of the Huey as it lifted off with two of the men who had recently joined him in this room of Satan's castle. Cursed with the full memory and experiences of MacMillan, Neil knew that six months had passed, and he was now considered an elder in the church of the platoon of brothers.

"Mac, can I talk to you?"

Neil watched the chopper move away before looking over at his commanding officer.

Lt. Abrams was flanked by Beanpole and the sergeant. "What's up, sir?"

The platoon had marched along the banks of a muddy river for the last three weeks. They had met resistance at every river bend and sandbar. They had lost half of their men in the last twenty-one days.

"Mac, we got our orders and it's some serious shit."

Mac/Neil nodded like it was just another day at the office. "What'cha not telling me sir?" He looked at the man—his father— and fought to hold his lunch down. He grabbed his cigarettes from his helmet and lit one, thinking that it would help settle his stomach.

The lieutenant looked from his sergeant to Beanpole and back to Mac. "We have a problem." Both Beanpole and the sarge stared snickering. Neil didn't like where this was going, or that he had to be a part of it.

"Yea? What's that sir?" Mac shuffled on his feet a little and reached out of habit for the grip of his M-16, which was slung across his back.

"I find myself in need of a sergeant," Abrams said, slapping the back of the sergeant standing next to him.

"I got my orders Mac! They're sending me Stateside to train newbies," the sergeant said, punching Neil in the shoulder. "I leave tonight."

"That's great Sarge!" Neil heard his Mac voice say in response.

"So, that leaves me without a sergeant," Lt. Abrams said flatly.

"They moved me to squad leader," Beanpole said, unable to contain his news as well.

"That makes you our new sergeant," Abrams said, handing over the new chevrons. "Congratulations. Now, come on, I need you two to help me plan this operation."

Over the next few days, Neil found himself settling into Mac's persona. Up to now, he had never had an *experience* that had lasted more than an hour. But now he was on his third day in someone else's body. The first night he crawled into his sleeping bag, he half expected to wake up next to Claire or next to the river—anywhere but here—but that didn't happen. Now, he found himself helping his father plan a raid on a high-value target in the middle of the Vietnam War. How this helped him answer the Old Man's question, 'why are you so angry', he would never know!

I'm not angry! I don't know what he's talking about?

"Did you say something Mac?" Abrams looked up from a map he had been studying for hours.

"Ah...no, sir. At least I don't think so. I guess my mind was someplace else."

The lieutenant leaned back in his chair and rubbed the palm of his hands across his forehead and what was left of the hair on his head before speaking. "Yea, I do that a lot as well."

Neil knew enough to let an officer talk without a response, but this was not just any officer, and there was a reason he was here. "Sir, if you don't mind me asking..." Abrams nodded. "What do you think about?"

In the short time Neil had been in Mac's soul, he knew that most men in Vietnam think about home. They think about hamburgers, cold drinks with ice, hot girls, and hot cars; and then there are some who think about their wives and the children that they left back home. You can see this level of thought on their faces. They carry a sense of worry, not of themselves, but what would happen to the ones they love. So, to move away from such dark places, they try and find places where the happy thoughts dwell. Once they get to this happy place, they don't want to leave. In this place, they can have the thoughts of normal people in a world that is anything but normal. In this place they can think about playing ball with their boy. They can think about taking their daughter out for a milkshake or they can think about watching a sunset with their wife at the beach. They think of the life that is on the other side of Hell's iron curtain; and most of all, they think of getting out of Vietnam...one way or another.

"It's a girl, my girl. We have a kid," Abrams said with a smile, while lighting a cigarette.

Neil felt the catch in his throat. In the six months that Mac had known Abrams, he had never mentioned anyone from home. War can take a lot from a man, but sometimes the man can choose to hold on to the things that keep him going. "How long have you been married?"

"Oh, we aren't married…yet." He put the cigarette down on the side of the table and leaned back in his chair, his eyes drifting away to another place. It had to be the happy place. "We didn't get a chance, you know? I was in college doing ROTC, and all of a sudden she was pregnant. It was our senior year, November to be exact; we didn't have that much more school left."

Neil studied the man. He soaked in his voice and tried to commit every war-born wrinkle and scar to memory. He could hear the voice of the real man, not the commanding office, but the voice of his father. He was hearing a man for the first time that he never thought he would hear. To Neil, this man was the source of so many problems in his life.

When Neil's father had returned from Vietnam he was changed physically and mentally. He had commitment issues and faded into and out of the lives of Neil and his mother.

But now, now his father was something different. He was someone that was strong and commanding. He was smart, cunning, and compassionate in his own way. This was the man that he had never really met until three days ago. Neil swallowed hard as he listened, trying not to well up. At least he didn't feel like throwing up anymore.

"I don't know, we were both working our way through school and then all of a sudden she was pregnant. We had nothing. No real place to live, no money, no real jobs. I know what you are thinking Mac," he said, pointing a finger at his sergeant. Neil shrugged slightly. "Why didn't we get married, right?"

Neil played along. "Sure." He was seeing the soul of the man exposed in front of him. Slowly, that soul had been let out of the dark place and was finally being allowed to speak. Neil knew the dark place, and was not shocked that his looked similar to his father's. Anger, drive, free will, are all things that can be passed down.

"Well, good question, but like I said, we had nothing, and the last thing I was going to do was go to our parents for help. They would've never understood, right?" He didn't wait for an answer. "They would have…they would have…well, it didn't matter because the army offered me money, a bonus to go into OCS without finishing school. I guess they were running low on lieutenants over here or something!"

"So, you took it. You…you didn't run from her being pregnant or something?"

They both stared at each other for a second. Neil felt like the man was going to come out of the chair and slug him. The anger that flashed across his face looked very familiar.

"No man, that's the last thing I wanted! I did it for us, and for our baby. I love her, and I love that baby. A boy! My boy! I loved him from the moment I saw him. You know what I mean, man?"

And there it was. Neil had carried around this anger and guilt the size of an iceberg his entire life, and it all had centered on this man, and these few words. He loved them.

Neil's father was sporadic at best in showing up in his life. Neil had spent a childhood bouncing between his grandmothers, and watched the constant absence of his father engulf his mother in misery. As Neil had aged, the man would drop into his life for a short time and then disappear, leaving Neil with a haze of misery and a sense of abandonment.

It was with these simple building blocks of abandonment and misery that Neil had constructed a wall of anger that served to undermine everything in his life. He could feel the emotion now and recognized what it for what it was—anger. An evil anger that consumed everything in its path, or in Neil's life. Even thought the Old Man had shown him many of the scenes of his life that were influenced by love, there were probably as many scenes that they did not visit that were sabotaged by anger. Was he right?

Why are you so angry? The words rattled in his head like buckshot.

But…but, now, with those simple words from his father, *"I love her, and I love that baby…I loved him from the moment I saw him,"* the wall…the wall that he had lived behind since childhood, showed the first signs of cracking.

"What," Neil felt his voice, dry from the moment, "What about the kid…what's happening with him?"

"The boy, he's awesome. He's named after me—Neil Abrams, Jr." The lieutenant stood up grinning ear to ear while pulling a plastic bag from his left breast pocket. In the bag was a small metal cross and a picture of why he was in the jungle. "He's staying with my parents while his mom finishes school."

Neil felt the blocks of his wall of anger, pounded by the weight of love, crack and crumble. Each of the blocks started tumbling away from around his soul. *Oh, dear God, I have been wrong my entire life!*

The realization of the confession from his father hit him so hard that he fought to catch his breath.

"Are you okay?" Abrams asked.

Neil looked at him square in the face, taking a second to drink in the man. He could feel that his time was ending. It was time to go back. "Yea, I am now."

< >

"He is a good man Neil." The Old Man said, breaking a long silence since the man had returned.

Neil was back along the river again. Safe. Safe from the Hell of war, but was he? With each step along the path and with each experience, he seemed to be moving further away from where he really wanted to be.

Neil heard the Old Man speaking to him, but another thought filled his mind. "This is the mission, isn't it? The mission that we were planning. It's the one that changes him...where he...he..."

"Loses his leg. Yes, this is the mission," the Old Man confirmed. "It is also the mission that starts him down a slippery slope of mental issues." The Old Man wrinkled his brow and seemed a bit misty-eyed. "I am so sorry."

Neil nodded. He knew the answer before he asked the question. But, he asked it anyway. "You're not going to let me go back and help him, are you?"

"No, son, I'm not."

"Why?"

"Because his journey takes a different path, a path that is different from yours, and it is one that you cannot change."

"But this mission, it changes everything. He loved me; he told me he did." Neil turned around to look to see if anything was changing around him...if he was back in Vietnam. It wasn't. "I didn't see him for years after he came home. I was almost seven...he came to one of football games. Are you sure I can't help him?" Neil felt the finality of the experience closing around his chest. He knew he wasn't going back. He had found the answer to the Old Man's question. It was time to move on.

The Old Man took in a deep breath. The plea seemed to move him, but his decision had been made at an earlier time. "Neil, this path is about you...you and me. You got to see that he loves you very much. His absence in your life wasn't about you, it was about him, and dealing with the demons in his head and the loss of his leg. That is his journey, his path to walk. Neil, this journey, the one we are on right now is about you. Son, I know you found what you needed. It is time to move on."

Neil struggled with what he had just learned; that his father had not abandoned him, that he had loved him and he had loved his mother. *He said it...leg or no leg...mental issues or not...he said it to me.* It would take him awhile, but he could find a way to use this experience to make his life better. And with that and the Old Man confirming that he had indeed found what he needed, he simply let the anger—the anger at the man, his father—simply fall away. The relief was enlightening and tiring all at the same time.

The Old Man recognized the change; the pivotal change that he needed. "Are you alright?"

Neil would always be hurt, but he was alright. He was tired and wanted one thing now more than any other...

"Can I go back to Claire?" Neil whispered.

There was a long silence from the Old Man as if he had not expected that response.

"Yes."

Neil nodded and stood up, the product of a changed man. "Good. Let's go."

The Old Man also stood and put his arms around the younger man.

Neil allowed the Old Man to support him. He felt secure and tired, and tried to hold back the first sob, but there was no holding back this level of relief. He began to sob uncontrollably and the Old Man wrapped his arms tighter around the younger man. Their journey together was coming to a close.

CHAPTER 13

Neil had been dozing. He cupped his hands to his face and rubbed his eyes trying to recall when the Old Man had released him from his sobbing. He felt a little better, but not really refreshed. He smiled into his hands and inhaled deeply, this time allowing his eyes to open slowly and his senses to acquire information. He was in a very familiar place.

The sensation of movement was present, as was the constant droning of engine noise. He could feel the touch of stable, dry air hitting the top of his head, and realization came at once. He started to move, but was strapped down, this time by an uncomfortable seatbelt, attached to an equally uncomfortable seat on an airplane…in coach!

"So, what was it?" Neil heard the lady sitting next to the window ask, pausing to look at the man sitting in the middle seat. She nudged him slightly, as he was flipping through pictures on his camera, obviously lost in the stories they held.

"What?" he asked, preoccupied.

"Nothing," she said lovingly, and then she also seemed to be pulled into the pictures. They made her smile. And then she seemed to remember that she had been talking across her husband to the man sitting in the aisle seat. "Sorry, where was I, oh yes, you had asked about how long we had been doing mission work," she said, smiling at Neil.

Neil looked at the lady, and then at the man, who was still flipping through the pictures. He felt the blood in his heart heat up and emotion fill every cell of his body, his skin tingled and popped as if every pore was about to emit sweat: He knew these people. But as the realization hit him, so did the compressed feeling of the cramped airplane. His breathing turned to short gulps as he strained to fill his lungs, his body convinced that the airplane had just run out of oxygen.

"So," the lady started again, this time looking into Neil's eyes. "Are you alright?" she asked tenderly. "Can I get you something, or call the flight attendant," she said, moving to press the button.

"Ahhh, no," Neil said, briefly looking into her eyes and just as quickly looking away; he suddenly felt sick to his stomach. "Excuse me a minute," he said, unbuckling his seatbelt and turning toward the back of the plane in search of the lavatory. His body felt different. He didn't move like the fit soldier he had been for the last few days, but instead he moved lethargically along the aisle, struggling to catch his breath and not cough.

Once inside the lavatory, he locked the bolt, activating the flickering light and held himself steady against the small elf-size sink. It was at that point that he looked into the mirror. What he saw looking back at him made his heart hurt. It was him. He was looking at himself, but it was a very different self than what he remembered.

He turned on the water and tried to catch a handful before the automatic shut off denied him his cupped hands fill. The water was lukewarm and smelled, but he splashed it on his face nonetheless. He let the water drip from his face and fall back into the sink. He rubbed his eyes and reached for one of the rough-hewn paper towels to wipe his face. And then he looked again, finding the same person looking back at him.

"Lord, what are you doing with me this time?"

And this time, he heard an answer. Quieter than the drone of the airplane, more tender than the crackling PA system, and bigger than the entire universe, he heard God's voice in his soul.

"Decide."

"What? What did you say? Decide? What does decide mean, Old Man?" Neil shook his head and looked at himself again, this time assessing what he really looked like. He was older, much older, or perhaps it was that he was carrying eighty or a hundred extra pounds that aged him so. He was sporting a full beard of gray and he had dark rings under his eyes. He was a mess…a mess of a person, and hard to look at. In his pocket he found a pack of antacids and with shaking hands he unwound the roll and popped two in his mouth. Also in the pocket was a business card, his business card, with handwriting on the back, his handwriting; "Remember to call Josh on his birthday…look up his number online." Neil flipped the card back over to see that he was a vice president of sales and marketing for an industrial manufacturer based in China. Neil shook his head, knowing that this was no badge of honor, but a testament to the sacrifice of his family…the one thing that he always said he didn't want to happen. Neil put the card back in his pocket.

Why here, why now?

He knew it had something to do with the couple sitting in his row. "What can they do for me? You have shown me my grandmothers, my life when we first started out, the horror of a suffering child in a country I have never been to before..." He wiped his face again, and looked up at the ceiling of the small bathroom ready to continue his litany. "You have driven me into the pit of Hell and told me to face my fear and find the source of my anger…Well I faced and found it, damn it…I get it, I was wrong, I am no longer angry, I forgive him. So what can these people on an airplane do for me that you have not already done?" Neil asked quietly of the mirror?

"Decide," the voice inside insisted.

He looked closer and deeper into the mirror, and into the eyes, the eyes of someone who did not seem to care and was tired of listening to the lessons that were so evident. "How did I get like this?"

Leaving the small confines of the lavatory, Neil aisle-danced his hefty body past disgruntled passengers crammed into their seats in search of his seat, but before he could make it, he was held up by the drink cart blocking his path. He was only a row or two from his seat. The flight attendant looked above the rim or her glasses to see the large man at the other end of her stainless steel cart. With a drink and a bag of peanuts in each hand, she held up a pinky finger in a gesture to get the large man to hold his peace for a moment while she finished.

Neil nodded and plucked a bag of the pretzels from the top of the cart. As he stood there munching, he quickly found himself lost in study of the couple from his row. They were blissfully unaware of his watching or even of anyone else on the plane; they seemed happy just to be there, with each other.

The man in the middle seat had moved from flipping through pictures on his camera and had produced a Mac computer to work on. Neil watched, as in a trance, the man happily dropped picture after picture into columns, after which he would type a quick description and then move the next picture into view; it looked as though he was working on a newsletter.

Finishing his small bag of pretzels, Neil crumpled the wrapper and looked down to wipe the salt and crumbs from his very wrinkled and traveled in shirt; he was a blob of uncaring style. He tossed the wrapper into the trash-bin on the cart and then really noticed what the people on his row looked like in comparison of himself. They were not blobs for starters!

The man in the middle seat was dressed in cargo pants and a wicking material shirt that seemed to fit his form well; he looked comfortable, in shape, and far from disheveled. His arms were tan, as was all of the other exposed skin; especially his bald head and the back of his neck. He seemed to smile and laugh a lot, always gesturing with his hands. To Neil, he was a character of commonplace, but with an undertow of commanding presence and a sense of quiet leadership.

Neil then turned his attention to the lady, and his heart skipped a beat. Even though he had spoken to her before getting up, he had not really looked at her. She was naturally beautiful, sporting blond hair pulled back into a simple ponytail. Like her husband, she smiled a lot, which was infectious. She wore dark yoga pants and a vibrant blue v-neck top. She wore a brown and blue set of Keen flip-flops and often bounced one of them off of her tanned foot as it dangled lazily across her leg. Every once in awhile, she leaned into the man to make suggestions or point to the screen as they happily created their work together. With nothing more than the minute of observation, Neil was jealous of the pair. They seemed well made and put together. They seemed happy and full of a life that Neil craved.

With little fanfare, the flight attendant finished serving the rows about her, kicked her parking brake off and pulled the cart out of Neil's way, allowing him to fall heavily into the leather seat with an *umph*.

"Feeling better?" the lady sitting next to the window asked kindly. "We didn't know what you might want, so we got you a tonic water, thinking that might help your stomach." She handed the bubbling drink across her husband to the large man.

"Thanks," Neil muttered, sipping slowly; but the chalky strawberry flavored antacid mixed with the cool bubbles of his drink turned his stomach into a cauldron of torment.

"Don't fly much, do you?" the man in the middle seat asked, never looking up from his computer.

"No, actually, I fly all of...the...time," Neil answered before he could really think, because in reality, before the accident, he did fly all of the time.

"Humm," the man in the middle said, "I used to as well; I had the frequent-flyer miles to buy us tickets anywhere, stay at the nicest hotels for free, and eat at fancy restaurants. But that's all changed. When I fly now, it's for a purpose, not a profit."

Neil soaked that in for a moment. How often had he told himself that if he just visited this customer or that customer that he would make his sales goal and ultimately a fat juicy commission? It was a little like the dogs in Pavlov's great experiment: ring the bell, take the flight, get your reward. Ring the bell, take the flight, take the flight, ring the bell.

Neil shook the thought from his head, the shadows of the word *Decide* still echoed around in his soul, trying to ground him. He knew he had to figure out why he was here and why now. Reassessing his thoughts, somehow, he knew that these people held the key for him; and that the questions he needed to ask were meant to help in ways he still did not understand. He cleared his head of his past experiences. He cleared the smell of death and Vietnam from his nose. He cleared his head about the accident that put him here. He cleared his head of the path that he walked with the Old Man. He cleared his head from the experience of his childhood and his son's birth, the death of his grandmothers, and the ultimate misery of a child at the side of the street. Instead, he focused on God. He focused squarely on God and His underlying grace. He focused on what His plan was for him and how he could make it a reality. He had seen so much in such a short time, and he felt that his answers were only a few questions, and a few seats away.

Decide.

A Bible verse came to mind just as he was about to speak. For Neil, Bible verses did not often come to mind. He was more likely to have remembered the Sunday reading, or the context of a conversation about the Bible with his Granny Lil, or watching Charlton Heston delivering the Ten Commandments, but never an actual verse from the Bible. The clarity of the words was unmistakable, and the voice he heard was that of an old man who walks a path. It was a quote from Mark, "For whoever wants to save his life will lose it, but whoever loses his life for Me will save it. What good is it for a man to gain the whole world, yet forfeit his soul."

With a sense of peace and a rapidly renewing focus, Neil reengaged the couple. "That is pretty good looking," he said, pointing a fat finger at the computer screen and opening himself up to what these two offered.

The man in the middle seat sat for a second, resizing a picture before answering. "Thanks, it's for our newsletter. About twenty-five thousand people see this each quarter, and I always want to make it right."

"So are you a publisher or work for *National Geographic* or something?" Neil asked slyly, knowing in his heart the real answer.

"No, we are both missionaries," the lady said, joining in.

"Well," the man in the middle seat piped in. "I never really thought of it that way." He looked over at his wife with a smile. "We also run a charity. We write books, host blogs, and take photos of our experiences. We help lead other faith-based groups to what we do and how they can help. We help young men and women find their place in life. Ultimately, we are like a mom and dad to hundred of kids, including our own. We do it all in the name of God, so, yea," he looked at his wife, "I guess we are missionaries." She smiled with an "I told you so" kind of look.

Neil processed what he was hearing, all the while stealing closer glances at these people, who seemed to exude happiness and have it all together. He did indeed know them, he knew them well, but they didn't recognize him, which made Neil sad, because they were vital to his life moving forward.

"What made you decide to do all of that, I mean the books, the speaking, the children, and all of that stuff. I mean to be missionaries and all?" he asked with a nod to the woman.

"Because there was one man that sacrificed himself so that we could have the choice, the choice to follow Him," the lady said, sure of her conviction. She said it with such strength and belief that it was almost a canned answer, which she seemed to sense once she said it. "Look, once we made the decision to follow the Lord, and our hearts, it was plain as day. All the rest of the stuff you worry about kind of fell away. We had a new focus."

"We are not religious nut cases or anything," the man in the middle seat added, "but we were given a gift that really changed our perspective. You talk about flying around the world and seeing things. Well, since I…excuse me, since *we* made the decision to follow Christ, we have been blessed to travel to places, to see things, to experience unbelievable events." He looked at his wife, who was smiling back at him and nodding, as she finished the thought.

"We have found more following God than we found following our former lives," she said, looking deep into his Neil's eyes. She seemed to be reaching into his soul to pluck the chords of Neil's heart. He felt the warmness of the wonder, the awestruck wonder of what it would be like to give up his former life and follow a new one under God's tutelage.

"That's true," the man in the middle seat said, breaking Neil's warm thoughts, "but it took some encouragement. Our lives were ones more of analyze and decide, wait and see, hold and wait for a better time; you know." Neil nodded like he did. "We were like college football coaches, you know the ones that sit up in the sky box. We would analyze the game, and based on what we saw coming, we would call in a play. We were never the ones on the field, making it happen, following a direction from someone that we couldn't see, but…but, that all changed with one event," the man in the middle seat said, ramping his voice down to a whisper. His vision seemed to lose focus as he stared in contemplative thought; the smiling faces of the pictures on his computer screen seemed to smile a little more, offering their encouragement.

With quiet trepidation, Neil slightly cleared his throat before speaking. "One event, what do you mean one event? How can all of your life pivot so sharply, and all of your happiness come from one event?" Neil questioned, but in reality, he knew what they were talking about.

"Well," the man in the middle seat seemed to pull back from his reflective thoughts and looked over at his wife again, possibly gaining strength to answer the question, or possibly just to ground his love, something that he would do until the day he died. "We were celebrating an anniversary, and times were tough. I had begged my family's mountain cabin for a long weekend and we left the kids with her parents and headed to the mountains."

"It was foggy," the woman offered, "and up until the accident," she bit her thumbnail nervously, "we had been arguing."

"What were you arguing about," Neil asked, void of the fact that there were hundreds of others on the plane; to him, there were only three souls onboard. He was locked into the story…a story that he knew.

"I don't know, something trivial…money, our business, I don't know," the man in the middle seat said. "I just had this disconnect in me that I couldn't get my head around. I didn't know what it was, but I was missing something and it was affecting me. I couldn't focus on work, on our family, on our Church, on God, on anything. This trip was a last try at holding onto sanity, and as usual Claire bore the brunt of my anger and self doubt; she was the only one who I could take it out on, she was the only one who understood. Like a true partner in life, she was sharing my disconnect…and so we argued."

Neil felt the last few sentences hit him like a pallet of bricks. He had never considered in his self persecution, in his self described disconnect, that it had all been his fault—the business failing, the lack of money, the kids going without, his anger at his father, the accident, his disassociation with God, would all be the turning point of their family.

Would they survive or fail as a couple…as a family?

Neil turned from the couple and with shaking hands downed the last of his drink. Deep breaths helped, but it was the touch of the lady that pulled him from his anxiety.

"Do you need something?" she asked, looking at him with eyes as blue as tropical oceans. "I am worried about you; should I check to see if there is a medic or doctor onboard?"

Neil looked into those beautiful blue eyes; she shared the same blue eyes as that of the Old Man on the path. Her eyes soothed him and reminded him of a time of happiness and confidence. He snapped back, remembering that he was there for a purpose.

"So, you were having a hard time, and your family, too," Neil said, swallowing his knowledge of the situation, and pressing forward with the questions.

"Yea, we were," the man answered, "but it all changed in an instant."

Neil looked at the man's face; he had still not looked up from the computer and met Neil face to face, but Neil knew him nonetheless. "Tell me about that, the moment it all changed I mean, the wreck."

The man in the middle seat fidgeted a bit, cracking his knuckles into fists, took a large breath, and exhaled. He was ready to talk. "We were bad off. I had lost my company and the economy was crashing. I didn't know what to do. We were both really involved in our church. We both served on different committees and actually helped guide the church in what we thought was the best direction—one of prosperity, outreach, and charity toward the youth and community."

"But as our business failed," the lady added, "we also failed. We were mad at the failure and blamed the church for not helping and God for not listening." She took a second to take a ragged breath. "I know it sounds weird, but we needed somewhere to put the blame, and especially after we had given so much…and…and…that's when…," a tear traced the side of her nose and fell onto a simple silver ring on her finger. The ring had a cross pressed into it, and the tear seemed to fill up the cross.

"That's when we had the accident," the man in the middle seat finished the sentence for her.

All three of them sat quietly as the weight of the statement sank in. Neil was keenly aware that the people around him had stopped talking; they were hushed in silent listening: Even the drone of the air vents seemed a little quieter. At that moment, his quest was their quest. The thought crossed his mind that perhaps he was not the only one on the airplane that might be searching for what God wanted from them?

"So," Neil ventured, breaking the quiet, breaking whatever other quests were out there, "what happened?"

"We chose to live," the man in the middle seat said simply.

Neil absorbed the effortless statement that contained complex implications. "How…how did you choose to live?" He was greeted with a long silence as the man in the middle seat thought through the answers.

"Well, for me, it wasn't simple, and it wasn't immediate. You see, I had to relive some things. I had to feel some things that I had not felt in a long time. I had to be reminded that I will never come up with a plan that is better than His, and because of that, had to feel some things that I had never felt. But…to really sum it up, I had to have a harsh talking to by my Father…a harsh talking to by God." The man smiled with a twisted kind of, *wouldn't want to do that again* grin.

Neil tossed that around for a minute, chewing on what it had been like to experience the harsh talking to by God. "Was He angry with you? What did He say to you, God I mean, what did he say, and how was it harsh? What did he do?" Neil spewed the questions fast, trying to process his experiences against what the man was saying.

"What did he do?" The man in the middle seat shook his head at the wonder of what He had done. "He did amazing things, things that shook my world, things that a mountaintop experience couldn't hold a candle to." The man sighed deeply again, thinking through the wonder. "You know, He showed me things that I had done, ways that I had strayed from the path, and the ways that I had not. He showed me innocence, love, hope, and hardship. He showed me that I matter to people that I don't even know…and to the people that love me more than I will ever know. He made me face my fears. He forced me to challenge my anger. He showed me things that were to come. He showed me the hope and the inspiration of just what can be. And He…well, He showed me how my life is important to my family, and how it's important to Him. He told me that I matter. But most of all, he taught me that I am loved by Him, no matter what I do." The man in the middle seat turned to look at Neil for the first time before speaking again. They locked eyes and studied each other's face before the man in the middle seat broke the silent stare with a hushed weighty tone of voice filled with passionate emotion. "In short, he showed me that I had a choice; a choice to accept the love He offers as a gift. He showed me that if I choose to spread the gift of love, that it turns into joy…and joy can quite simply be overwhelming!"

Neil swallowed hard thinking back through the recent events since the accident. *Was this the culmination? Was he now faced with* the *choice? All of the things that I have seen…they have all been for* this *choice.* Neil's throat was dry. "So, even after showing you all of that…He still gave you the choice to accept His love or not?" He was having a hard time believing all of this, even though he had been through it all himself.

"Finally," the man in the middle seat continued without answering the question. "I was shown an incredible amount of grace. And you know what?" He pointed a finger at Neil. "Grace is at His very essence. It is! It was beautiful you know. He actually showed that to *me*." He turned the finger on himself poking his chest with animation, "He showed me that my life has been filled with a current of underlying grace. He said that I am important to His plan. His plan! Go figure!" The man shook his head again in slight disbelief. "You know, He showed me that I had a pivotal hand in the survival and growth of my family. He gave me a choice about accepting His love, and He forced me to make a decision about how I was going to live my life. And," the middle-seat man looked Neil squarely in the eyes, "if I was going to offer advice to someone about making that decision," he raised his eyebrow at

Neil. "The decision to live my life accepting His love and impact others in His name. I'd tell them to say *yes!*"

Decide

With chill bumps spreading across his skin, Neil heard the voice, the advice of the middle-seat man reverberating in his soul.

The man in the middle seat nodded as if he also had heard the word *decide* in his head. "I did, I had to decide what to do. I needed to decide. I wasn't going to survive this accident and still be my old self. Someone filled with self-doubt and pity, anger and resentment. *No!* If I was going to do this, I was going to embrace life, create a more vibrant story and live life to the full extent of God's grace!" The man in the middle seat turned to smile at his wife, who laced her arm in his and held him a little closer. Tears were now flowing freely from her eyes.

"We chose the second life, and although sometimes road bumps pop up along the way, we have never...ever...regretted turning our lives over to God and what His plan had in store for us," she said, gently squeezing his hand and exchanging a small kiss.

"Excuse me sir," a woman said, tapping Neil's shoulder. He looked up to see the flight attendant waiting patiently in the aisle.

"Yes."

"I have this for you from a gentleman in first class," she said handing him a tall cold drink and a small white piece of paper.

"Ahh, thanks," he said, taking the paper and drink, miffed that he had been interrupted at the crux of this story. The drink was in a tall glass; two shades of tan liquid had separated about mid point in the glass, and bits of peach floating up and down like lava lamp bubbles. Neil tasted it and the flavors of peach followed by a sweet syrup taste zinged the hinges of his jaw and instantly put his stomach at ease. He had had one of these before, and there was only one place in the world where you could get it. He took the paper and unfolded its message.

Please come to seat 1A.

Neil read the paper a few times and then looked at the couple sitting next to him, conflicted with what he should do.

"You should go to Him," the man in the middle seat said without looking at the paper.

Neil shot him a look of shock, but after the events of his day, this was nothing all that unusual. With no further courtesy, he palmed his drink, stood, and plodded down the aisle, pushing aside the sheer blue curtain of first class to find an empty seat waiting for him in row 1. The man sitting in 1B wore an explorer's hat, but it was the cargo pants, blue shirt, and the gray hair that showed who he really was.

CHAPTER 14

"So, I said I want you to see a few more things before you start making choices," the Old Man said, as white clouds whisked by at airplane speed outside the oval window.

Neil plopped rudely in the empty seat, strangely unaware of the heft that he still carried.

"How do you like the drink?" the Old Man asked.

Neil took another sip, this time sucking in more of the peaches. "You know I have had one of these before." The Old Man turned to him and raised an eyebrow that said, *really*!

"I thought I was there, before you sent for me. I mean, I think I know what my answer is," he expelled, ignoring the older man's sarcasm and blurting before he could really think. For some reason, Neil was suddenly nervous. It was almost like being called out by Mr. Miyagi after doing the bird kick wrong in *Karate Kid*. Neil had to try to remember what he was learning; this is His plan, not mine. "Wax on. Wax off."

"You have not yet found the real reason why you will make the decision you will make," the man said simply.

"Well," Neil stuttered. "Well, what am I supposed to do? I thought I was there; I faced my anger, I relived the torment of my youth, I was having a great conversation with my other," he looked down at his belly, "more attractive self, and then you called me up here!"

"That is an interesting choice of words," the Old Man said, zeroing in on one part of the rant. "That I called you," he said turning to face the fat man. "I have definitely called you; you just need to hear what I am saying and choose to follow what I am saying. In your thoughts, you want to circumvent my plan; you have done so many times in the past. You always know better! But, this is not your fault alone. I bear some of the burden."

"I...I don't understand? After sitting back there and listening, I am ready to make the decision!"

The Old Man pushed his hat up on his head a bit, scrunching his forehead as if thinking through what he was about to say. "Well, for you and for most people, it is not that they don't choose to hear me, it is that they can't separate my voice from all of the other noise in their lives. It's like earphones that block out all noise and create invisible bubbles—force fields around them—protecting them from the influence of others. People, especially the kids, spending time talking to a computer and measuring their popularity by the tally of people that have clicked a computer mouse in allegiance. Friends are not numbers to be collected, they are people that love you."

Neil sat quietly as the Old Man seemed to want to get this off his chest.

"Neil, this journey is about you, but what you did not see for so long is that I have been part of the journey. Like fabric laced on the tapestry of your life, I am here to hold you and guide you. But, I am finding it harder and harder to get that idea through to men and women now," the Old Man said, sighing deeply. "I will adapt and still get my message through, I always have, but I also need to find a way for people to be open to hearing my message before something else fills the void. I am competing against the forces of free will, and sometimes I lose…it happens."

Neil finished the drink, letting the ice clink to the bottom of the glass. He was not sure if he needed to comment or not. His indecision seemed to bring the Old Man back around to his primary mission.

"So, you said you think you know what your decision is and that you have this whole thing figured out?" the Old Man said, suddenly back in the game.

"I...I think so."

"Good, I also want you to be aware that the time to make that decision is nearing, and that this vision, all of this," he waved his hand around slightly and the air seemed to vibrate like ripples on a still pond from a tossed rock, "will end soon, and then you *must* make a decision. But," he cautioned, "not before it gets harder."

"I don't know how much harder it can get, but I will follow you," Neil simply said.

"Good, son, I knew you would. Now why don't you head back to your seat, and you might want to ask that fine couple about what they are doing now."

Through a few bumps of turbulence, Neil found his original seat next to the couple. He shook his head as to why he was actually summoned up to the front, and with that, he fell into the tight confines, reaching for the seatbelt, and noticed that it had a belt extender attached to it. He huffed heavily, clipped in, and adjusted the air vent.

"Sometimes He just wants to check in with us," the man in the middle seat said to his heavy friend, not looking up from his computer.

"You have no idea," Neil remarked sarcastically, as he watched the man in the middle seat work on the newsletter again.

"Think so, huh?" the middle-seat man said, smiling to himself.

"So tell me more about what you guys do now," he said, suddenly remembering the last thing the Old Man had said to him.

The woman sat up a little and looked at the large man sitting next to her husband. "So, about five years ago, we started a nonprofit in Honduras that helps teenagers. Our students already have a primary education, and we help them take the next step to becoming a productive citizen of their country."

Neil nodded approval, and the man in the middle seat clicked a file closed and took up the conversation again.

"Claire works with the boys and girls, teaching them life skills such as how to open a bank account, how to manage money, interviewing for a job, creating resumes, renting an apartment, grocery shopping, and giving back to the community. It was all her idea and passion." He winked at his wife, and she smiled back at him. "I also work with the kids, but I get to use my influence as a former industrial executive to help place the kids in work environments. We leverage those connections traveling to the States to solicit corporations for scholarships and apprentice positions. Finally, I get to do what I really love; I get to write about our experiences. It is great! From a third-world country I use modern technology to write the blogs, manage the social media, and submit news articles. We have thousands of followers that support us through their voices and their donations. Finally, we both travel and speak to organizations about our passion and how they can help."

"His third book about our experiences with these wonderful people will come out next month," Claire said, beaming at her husband. "We now have two schools," she continued. "We call them Pads, like launch pads. It also stands for Passionate Action (through) Devoted Service. See, here it is, she said, grabbing her husband's hand resting on the mouse and clicking a logo on his computer showing the PADS logo.

To Neil, the graphic of children laughing under a blue sky and rainbow with a cross embossed across it seemed to hit home. He had had this very image in his head for a long time.

"We're working on our third school," she continued. "This time in Belize and perhaps one in Panama in two years." She said suddenly realizing something. "You know, I am sorry, we've done all the talking." She giggled softly. "We do that a lot. We're so passionate about what we do. So, I'm sorry, and what is it that you do?" she asked, not really understanding that she was stepping on his throat with the question.

Decide

Neil ignored the voice while trying to think of something that sounded remotely meaningful or compelling. Instead, his mind found inconsequential memories of the life of a road warrior. He found a mind full of memories of the version of himself that he currently occupied. These weren't his memories. But still, he could see places and things in his head. Places he had gone without his family, places where a meeting was held, or a customer's factory. He had nothing. In his current form, his memory told him that since the accident his life had been one of pain and regret. And then the worst memory of all surfaced -- his wife had died in the hospital.

She just never woke up. Her injuries were too extensive and she just never made it back. Even though he had lived, he had died partially when he lost her.

After the accident, he had given up on everything—his kids, his family, and his friends. He actually remembered telling God that he was not able to do what he needed to do; he was done. So, he threw in the towel and gave up on life. And twenty years later, this is where he was—an overweight traveling salesman on the verge of a heart attack and with nothing to live for.

"I'm in sales," he finally said to the lady, the lady that had been his wife all those years ago. He had almost forgotten what she looked like. She was still so naturally beautiful nearly twenty years later.

"Oh," she said, sitting back a little in her seat.

"Road warrior huh?" the man in the middle said, again not looking him in the eyes. He was sizing a picture, an old picture of a younger version of the woman sitting next to him, and a teenage boy.

"Josh," Neil said under his breath. He had not seen his kids in years, after losing the custody hearing with Claire's parents.

The man in the middle glanced over to see that the large salesman was staring at his computer screen. He turned his computer so that he could see the images better. "I am working on a chapter for my next book. It is really about all of the successes, all of the kids that we have been blessed to help." He pointed to the screen. "The lady there is my wife, the young man is my son when he was seventeen..."

"He runs his own mission now. He helps start companies in Central America by finding microloans to upstart homeless children that have dreams of building businesses." Claire said, beaming with pride.

"That he does," the man in the middle seat continued. "So like I was saying, this is my wife, this is our son Josh, and they are both holding two children."

"Brother and sister," Claire added.

"Right, they were rescued by Claire and Josh while on a Mission trip in Honduras."

"They were living in a pile of trash on the side of a dirt road. Both their father and mother had died," Claire said, the rims of her eyes watering with emotion again.

Neil knew them.

"After the car crash that changed our lives we knew that we had a higher purpose, and finding these two children helped us solidify what we were to do about it." He then moved a second picture of Claire, a recent one, across the screen and next to the older one. She had one arm around a medium height man with jet-black hair and the other arm around a teenage girl. Before he said anything, Neil knew who they were—he had been that boy once.

"Pablo and Nince," Neil said quietly. Neither the man in the center seat or his wife questioned how he knew their names; but both smiled knowingly with a quick glance at each other.

"You see, these children were some of the first kids to go through our school. We do what we love because of kids like this. It is our calling."

"It's our passion. We live for this kind of life," Claire finished.

Neil swallowed hard. Had it been right in front of him this entire time? Why had he resisted? Why was he resisting even now? *This is a no brainer decision*, Neil thought as the man in the middle seat turned to look at him again.

Neil let him study his face, and he could tell looking into his own eyes, the eyes of the man that had made the right decision, the eyes of the man that was living life to the fullest. These were the eyes of a man that had found God's Grace.

"You know, I was you at one time," he said smiling with understanding.

Neil didn't have a response. He simply nodded to allow the other Neil to talk, and perhaps tell him what he should do.

"You have been given a gift, a glimpse at what could be. All of this, everything you have seen, the conversations you have been having with our old friend," he said, nodding toward first class. "We know each other Neil," the man in the middle seat said looking the other man right in the eyes. "I know the position you are in. I remember how hard it was and I want you to know that you can make it better; I want you to fight for what you truly are. Fight for the man you can be. Fight for your family. Fight for your wife. Fight for kids like these." He pointed to the screen. "This Neil, is the decision that God is asking you to make. Accept the love. Pass it on."

All along, Neil had thought this journey, this walk along the path of his life, this emotional roller coaster he was on with the Old Man, would really be about a question of if he wanted to live or die...and, in a lot of ways it was. The accident had put him in a position in which it would be easy to choose death. The Old Man had told him several times that he had to make a choice, a decision, a step one way or another. Even after all of the visions and the emotional churning up of the seabed of his soul, he had felt all along that the decision would be a simple one, an easy choice, the path of least resistance. He would choose to die, to go ahead and go to Heaven. It had to be better than what was out there for his life. He was a failure and there was no climbing out of that hole, right?

In his mind, before the wreck, his life had been a wreck. He was in a tailspin in life. He was dragging his wife, their marriage, his relationship with the kids, and everyone around him down to the murky confines of self-pity and personal torture. Sure, the Old Man had shown him the highlights, but…but.

But here he was, looking at what the upside of the coin looks like. This man and woman had chosen heads and moved on to dominate the game. It must be hard to fail when God is calling the plays! *He has shown me all of this for a reason.*

"Excuse me sir," the flight attendant tapped him on the shoulder again, holding a note in her hand like last time. Without grace, Neil took the note, not really looking at the message, but he knew where he must go. He chose to focus his last seconds on what he really wanted to know.

"So, really the question is?" Neil asked the middle-seat version of himself. "It's not that you had a choice to survive the crash. You were going to do that anyway. It's the choice to live life—to really live life—to follow the path that God put in front of you…right?"

Neil glanced at the note: "I want you to meet someone, please come to me."

CHAPTER 15

Neil held the stare of the man in the middle seat for almost a minute. Each man conveyed libraries of information across the beams of their sight. One telling the other what he should know, one telling the other one that he was still not completely sure.

Neil broke the uneasy stare and lifted his hefty frame out of the leather chair to answer the call of his latest note. Really unsure of why he was being summoned to the front again, and actually pretty angry that it was interrupting the conversation with the man in the middle seat. Neil reached up and pulled back the blue curtain separating the cabin, but instead of the fine leather seats or faces of pampered passengers, what he saw blew his mind.

Neil was outside; it was suddenly hot and very arid. He looked behind him, and the fake leather seats of coach with integrated entertainment systems had dissolved into hard benches hued from rich trees. He looked down at his hands; they were his normal hands. In the swipe of a curtain moving back and forth, he had been changed back to his former size and age. Very much like a magician would swoop his silk cape over an illusion; you expect one thing, but you see another.

The sun, the beautiful warm sun, washed his face and flooded his eyes, preventing him from seeing the details that surrounded him. He put his hand up to block the glorious light as he sidestepped into a shadow trying to figure out just where on earth he was. The shadow was the first thing that he noticed.

He was standing in a massive shadow, and it had a very distinctive shape. It was not one of a giant oak or a shimmering pine, but was human, a massive human. But this shadow bore soft features, inviting coolness and a presence that fell across him like a picnic blanket on a warm day in the park. He looked up at what was casting the shadow and his breath caught. It was a statue, a beautiful giant statue. "I know where I am," he whispered to himself, suddenly remembering the significance of the peach drink from earlier…*you can only get them here!*

Wonderstruck, Neil smiled at the realization that he had been here… "But, why here?" He looked up at the beautiful white statue of the Virgin Mary. He began to move his feet; he was drawn to her beauty, to her aura, but most of all, he was drawn to her radiance of pure love. Perched at the crown of a mountain that overlooks the scenic city of Santiago, Chile, the hundred-foot statue of the Holy Mother calls people from around the world to climb the mountain, to come in peace and to worship on Her holy ground.

Neil had climbed this mountain before. Several years earlier, during a business trip, he had taken some personal time to see some of the sites of this vibrant and inviting city. One of the things on his short bucket list was to hike up to the top of the mountain and see the statue. What he had not realized was that on the day he had chosen to walk up the five-mile trail in the state park, so had tens of thousands of other people. A holy day in the Catholic Church sent a call across the land for people to pilgrimage to the top to see the Holy Mother and kneel in prayer at her feet.

Neil had let the wave of people pull him along the state park like a river flowing up hill. He felt as one with the people; although he towered over them in height and his skin was a different color, he was welcomed as a child of God. The day had been hot, almost too hot for the North American tourist. Coming very unprepared for the hike, he had stopped halfway up to remove his T-shirt and use it as a bandanna. The November sun is hot in South America!

Now alone, Neil moved slowly up the final stairs to stand at the base of the statue. The concrete was slick with wax from the tens of thousands of prayers that had been offered to the saint, all of which were sent adrift with the flame and smoke of a symbolic white candle. The area was peaceful, and he was the only person in sight.

Neil picked up his own candle and lit it from an eternal flame. He looked at the flicker of the light and then up to the Virgin. This was the first time that he had thought about praying since he started his walk with the Old Man. The thought warmed him. He felt tired and worn, but something told him that he was nearing the end of his walk, and soon he could rest one way or the other.

He knelt at the railing, setting his candle in a wax-strewn iron grate that more resembled a dribble castle made of wax than an iron grate. He closed his eyes, bowed his head and his mind instantly flooded with the images of his walk. He could see the rhythmic flashing of the lights on the emergency vehicles bouncing off of the fog from his wreck. He felt the straps across his legs from when he had had the privilege to be with his grandmother during her last minutes. He could feel the crunch of grit between his teeth from when he was a homeless boy in Central America. He could smell the mud from where he had been lost in the reeds. His skin came alive with the heat from the napalm and his heart filled up from when he had relived the moment he asked Claire to marry him. With this as a backdrop, he began to pray:

"Lord. Dear God. I have sinned. I know I have. I have carried the pain of anger around with me my entire life. I have not loved when I was loved. I gave up when I should have stood up. Dear Lord, I ask that you forgive me. I beg for your forgiveness. I don't want to be the person that you showed me I could become.

"I want to be the person that lives the life you gave me to live! I want to serve in your name! I want to be joyful that I am loved by you, and the people that you have placed along my path. Lord, I am not through walking the path. I am not through living my life. And Lord, I want to do the work you want me do. Lord, you are a crazy old man that has shown me that I need to enjoy your gifts, your humor, your challenges, and your love! You have shown me that love can indeed conquer all, and that I must base the rest of my life on this simple truth." Neil breathed in deeply and exhaled. *"I love you dear God. I thank you for healing this disconnect in*

me. I thank you for filling it with love, and opening my eyes to the glory of the people that share that love with me; but most of all, dear God, I have made my decision, and I want to continue on this path of life...I want to accept your love and serve you! Amen."

"Amen." Neil heard a man's voice next to him say in agreement.

Neil opened his eyes and turned his head to the man who was kneeling beside him. The man was robed and hooded like a monk, or priest in simple vestments. The man raised his head from his own prayer and lifted his arms to remove his hood. Neil felt a catch in his throat as the man's bearded face was revealed.

"Jesus?"

"Yes my son."

CHAPTER 16

Neil lowered his head toward the man.

"My son, please rise; let us walk together," Jesus said, reaching out and touching Neil's shoulder. Neil felt a sense of calm and peace flood through his body from the touch. He stood and they both started walking slowly, almost aimlessly.

"You have done very well walking the path with my Father. Reliving such raw emotions and situations can make or break a man. It can take a toll on your soul. I am proud of you."

"Thank you my Lord," Neil said, his voice smooth and measured. He was thankful for the calmness of the touch on his shoulder: otherwise he was sure that he would be a blundering fool. His mood was blissful and talking to this man, the greatest man that had ever lived on earth, left Neil in a dreamlike stupor.

"Please call me Teacher," Jesus offered.

Neil smiled at the title; he had always seen Jesus as a leader, a source of inspiration, a well of hope, a person that could instruct…a teacher. Neil shook the dreamy feelings from his consciousness and tried to concentrate. He had no idea where this conversation was going to lead.

"Teacher, when I prayed, just then, I asked to continue my life, to step off my current path and to step on another one, one that has meaning. Is…is that going to happen?"

"Yes Neil, it will, but first, my Father has asked that I speak with you about your gifts; your gifts from our God." Neil nodded quietly, as the Teacher stopped walking and looked up at the face of his mother on the grand white statue.

"You know," Neil offered, "I did not grow up knowing how important your mother is to millions of people in the world." Jesus never took his gaze off of her, but instead let the man speak. "I mean that with no disrespect, Teacher, but you and your father are at the center of our…of my worship." Neil felt the calmness ebbing away. *Where am I going with this?* "But, I guess what I am trying to say is that, as I've grown older, and hopefully a little wiser, I'm trying to say that I have seen how your mother is central to so many things. Her bravery, her commitment to God, her strength, her…"

"Love," Jesus said, turning to Neil with a warm smile.

"And especially her love."

"And that is precisely why my father wanted me to speak with you Neil." They started walking slowly again, away from the setting sun and slowly away from the great statue. "You have every one of those gifts, the same ones that my mother has. You have bravery, strength, a commitment to God, and love, but it is what you do with these gifts that will please Him the most."

"Yes Teacher," was all that Neil could utter.

"The man on the airplane, the version of you and Claire, that is only one outcome for your life. It is a glimpse of what could be when you combine these talents and trust in God's plan for you."

"You mean I can do other things?" Neil was briefly confused. "You mean that wasn't the only thing I can be?" Neil stopped talking, thinking how dumb he sounded. "Don't get me wrong, they…I…it's a beautiful existence, I would be honored to serve Him that way." *I am such an idiot!* "I'm sorry Teacher, I don't understand."

"Free will is one of the gifts from our God," Jesus continued, "and free will can be the lead weight or the catalyst when coupled with the gift of love. So, yes, Neil, you can have the outcome you saw on the airplane…either man's outcome—the man that you want to be, or the man that you did not want to be. The only difference between the two men was how they chose to use the gifts of love and free will."

Neil felt the power of the lesson wash over him as all of the pieces of the walk with the Old Man started to come together. Every time he was part of a different experience, it involved a decision, a right or a wrong, a yes or a no, an action of free will. Also, it always involved love or trust, or belief; and every one of the decisions…

"Was influenced by God," Jesus finished Neil's thought for him. "He gives you the gifts, and like a good father, tries to help you use them to the best of your abilities. Do you understand?"

Neil nodded that he did understand. "Thank you. Thank you both for what you have done for me," Neil said, the water of salty tears making their first appearance in several hours.

"Neil, you are blessed and I love you."

Neil fell to his knees, lowering his head as the love from the man filled him with a joy that is only fully understood in Heaven. His tears of joy flowed and rolled down his face without hindrance. "Thank you…thank you," he whispered in between the sobs of joy. Neil felt a hand touch his shoulder. The touch was reassuring and transmitted love. He knew that he was to rise.

When Neil stood, instead of looking into the face of the Son, he was now looking into the face of the Old Man…the Father. Neil embraced him with a deep hug that filled his heart with peace and hope.

"Son," the Old Man said, returning the hug, "you are special to me and I want you to know that I am proud of you and that I love you very much."

Like any child that has been loved and appreciated, Neil felt like he could do anything. He could sense the change in his body, mind, and spirit. He was ready to face whatever he needed, he was ready to do God's will and walk a meaningful path of life.

"Son," the Old Man said, pulling Neil to arms length to look at him.

"Yes my Lord," Neil said, pulling himself together. He was beaming and awash with Heaven's holy glow.

The Old Man simply turned Neil around. "Walk forward, son. I will be here for you."

Neil was looking at an evening fog bank that rolled with purpose. There was nothing to look at, and he was about to say so, when he thought he saw something move in the fog. Neil felt the hands, the powerful hands of his Lord, release him with a slight push to walk toward the fog. Neil took a few tentative steps, his vision fine-tuning with every inch forward…and that is when he heard her.

"Neil? Neil, is that you?"

"Claire! Oh dear God, thank you!" he started to run. "Claire!"

CHAPTER 17

They fell into each other's arms surrounded by the love and knowledge that they would never let each other go again. They were each crying so hard that neither could speak. Neil kept pushing back her blond hair and kissing her tear-stained face. Claire kept nuzzling into his chest, finding her safe harbor. Time stood still for the two, neither one wanting to let the other go.

"Neil and Claire," the Old Man said, from a few feet away. "I have enjoyed our time together, but, as you both have arrived at the same decision, it is now time for you to go."

It took a minute, but the statement started to pierce Neil's consciousness, and slowly he turned his body, still holding Claire tightly, so that they could see the smiling face of the Old Man.

"What do you mean we've both arrived at a decision?" Claire asked before Neil could get the question out.

"Were you walking the path, too?" Neil asked looking down at Claire.

She simply nodded, and smiled, and started crying happy tears again, gently nuzzling her head into his chest. He kissed the top of her head, feeling his own tears recharging for another round.

"Children," the Old Man said, coming to put his arms around them, "I will give you both a lifetime to sort this one out. Besides, I know for a fact that you both have a lot of talking to do. From the sound of your prayers, you two are only just beginning something very special."

Claire reached out and gently cupped her hands around the Old Man's face and pulled him down so that she could kiss him on the forehead.

"Thank you," Neil mustered.

"It is my pleasure." He beamed. "Now, I need you both to pull yourselves together, I have one final place for you go…and it requires your immediate attention," the Old Man said, stepping aside and urging them to walk deeper into the fog.

Neither one moved until Neil tightened his grip on Claire's hand, and slowly they started to walk past the Old Man and into the fog.

"Just remember children, that I am here, I am always here for you."

Neil turned his head to catch a glimpse of the Old Man before the fog swallowed him. The glimpse settled him and he knew he was ready, with Claire by his side, for anything and especially for the rest of their life together.

< >

Neil turned his head back to where they were headed and instead of trees and fog, he saw the glow of the dashboard on his Suburban. He was holding the wheel with both hands and driving the two-ton vehicle just as he had seconds before the accident. Claire reached up to change the station as it faded to static, but something else caught her attention. On her wrist, she was wearing the second half of a seashell, bound by the string of an old kite. She touched the shell, knowing that it had all been real. She reached for Neil's hand.

"Do you think the kids are okay?" she asked as if she had already asked the questions in a prior time.

It was like a key opening the floodgates of one's experiences. At that instant they both knew what had just happened to them…everything—every fear, hope, expectation, loss, and love. They had shared the experience but had been apart. Neil reached his hand out for his wife with love that he had not felt in years and she took it with an equal amount of love. They had an instant to share the experience as soul mates before their lives changed…this time for good.

Neil was looking at his wife when out of the corner of his eye he glimpsed evil coming after them. Not unlike what he had seen in

Vietnam, or on the other side of a counter from his grandmother. This evil was unpredictable and wanted to consume them. In one motion Neil jerked his head back around while slamming on the brakes. The offsetting action of the all wheel drive on the slick road and the over correction by Neil was working to save them. In the instant that he could analyze the trajectory he could see that they were going to go into the other side of the ditch at best. Not the best outcome, but better than striking the rig head on.

But what Neil could not see is that the driver of the eighteen-wheeler, a man of nearly thirty-two years of age, had been drinking with friends at one of the local truck stops at the top of the pass. What Neil could not see was that the same man, whose name was Billy, had decided that if he took the hit off of the crack pipe he could power through his next 120 miles and get back on schedule. What Neil could not see was that Billy's heart had been weakened by the constant up and down on his body as he tried to pick himself up to make the extra miles, and drink himself back down with his favorite whiskey. And finally, what Neil could never have known was that tonight, just an eighth of a mile earlier, Billy's heart had practically exploded under the competing forces in his body, killing him instantly and leaving his truck traveling down the winding road on its own.

Evil is unpredictable.

Neil changed feet and stomped on the gas, spinning the tires toward the other side of the road, and that is when the eighteen-wheeler suddenly jerked violently back toward the Suburban. It was at that point that he thought he heard Claire's screams, and could still feel her hand on his leg, gripping for safety.

The truck and trailer jackknifed and flipped on its side with such violent force that tires and metal parts exploded in all directions. The back end of the trailer followed the path of least resistance and began to swing around to the left side of the road, where it pushed out over the edge of the ditch at a high rate of speed—exactly where Neil had been angling the SUV.

Neil looked at the panic on his wife's face, but could also see that she was praying. Time seemed to slow down. He watched the cab of the rig slide by his wife's window with sparks flying off the road like a welding torch.

The high beams of the Suburban illuminated the top of the trailer an instant before the front end of their SUV collided with it, spinning it around the wreckage. They bounced into the ditch and rolled across the other side. Neil sensed the airbags deploying, and then he saw the ice in his iced tea cup fly straight up and suspend there while the suburban rolled in the air. The ice suddenly changed directions smashing into the front window as it shattered, and then he heard Claire scream again. Somehow his hand found hers as they rolled, and he too screamed out. He screamed out to God.

CHAPTER 18

Neil stood on the third floor of a simple building in Tegucigalpa, Honduras. He was looking out of the window at a world that would have been alien to him five years earlier. Simple box homes stacked on top of each other, held together by hardened clay, strips of rusted tin, and sheer will, provided the backdrop across the beautiful mountains that surrounded the city.

His building stood at the edge of a new technology park. Housing several North American tech companies, the park served as a beacon of the future for the city and its people.

Using his business experience, Neil had spent several years consulting with some of the companies that now operated in the technology park. His walk with God had shown him that not everyone has to drop their life and go be a missionary in Africa. *Although, I came close!*

Once he and Claire had recovered from the wreck, they spent the next six months dreaming, researching, evaluating, studying, and throwing a lot of ideas against the wall to see what would stick. They also did a great deal of praying. Something that used to be hard for them now became second nature.

Prayer led them here, to a small building at the edge of society in a third-world country.

Once they knew they had the right collection of ideas, passion, support, and love, they mixed it all together to pour the new path of their life; a path that God had helped them cast and create.

For Neil, the path allowed him to slowly divest himself away from the hectic sales management role he was in and ebb into a two-pronged career. Each side allowed him to do what he loved, and both sides served God. One day, he would pen a magazine article, write a blog, or work on his second book. The next day, he would work with the corporations, helping them design and implement charitable programs.

All the while as he changed his path, so did Claire. Neil's unofficial third job was helping her and the rest of the family start something small that, eighteen months later, had grown into something big. *So here we are in Honduras.*

Claire had found the resources and backers to help them start their mission to help train and integrate boys and girls into life and work after high school in a place where most people can't write their name. It was a transition program that filled the gap between what they had learned and what they needed to know in order to be successful at the next step in life. She had even found the time, space, and resources necessary to carve out a smaller mission, where the organization provided childcare for young unwed mothers so that they could continue their education. She called the entire program The GAP Mission, which spoke to its purpose and also to what the letters actually meant—God Always Provides.

From the third floor window, Neil watched his son, Josh, on the street below; unload one of the GAP vans with supplies. Josh had been in the country for the last three years. His Spanish was flawless, and he had the knack for moving from one culture to the other with ease. Using his international business degree and his sheer talent, he had established an outreach program between the businesses in the tech park and the surrounding community. He had found his calling.

Neil watched as four or five of the boys from Claire's program rushed out of the building to help his son unload the van. Feeling the need to help them as well, Neil turned and walked through the upper floor, which was filled with personal computers. Hector, one of the boys that had graduated from the GAP program, was writing on an active board connected to the computers. He smiled at Neil, and then went back to his preparation for teaching a class on creating a resume.

Neil patted him on the shoulder and made his way down through the practical life floor, where young ladies were learning math from an American volunteer. Once on the bottom floor, he was stopped in his tracks by a beautiful display of love.

Claire was leaning against a doorframe looking into a room filled with the young children of the day-care program. The light of the day lit her frame in a way that made his heart fill with love. He quietly walked up behind her, slipped his arm around her waist, and looked at what had captured her attention.

"Careful, she just might end up liking it here," Neil whispered to her.

Their daughter, Kat, was sitting in the middle of a gaggle of children reading to them in perfect Spanish. The richness of her story played across the faces of the children, each one hanging onto every word. Claire reached around the doorframe and kissed her husband on the cheek.

"I love you," she whispered.

"I love you, too."

"You know what?" Claire asked, wheeling herself toward Neil's embrace.

"What?"

"I think the kids are going to be okay."

We have different gifts, according to the grace given us. If a man's gift is prophesying, let him use it in the proportion to his faith. If it is serving, let him serve; if it is teaching, let him teach; if it is encouraging, let him encourage; if it is contributing to the needs of others, let him give generously; if it is leadership, let him govern diligently; if it is showing mercy, let him do it cheerfully.

-- ROMANS 12: 6-8

I think that God gives us more love than we can ever use, so go out and share it with people that don't know that God gave them love, too.

-- G. Allen Mercer

ACKNOWLEDGMENTS

I would have a hard time making a full list of the people who have helped me construct this story. I can say that one day, when I thought the end was near for what I was doing, I had this overwhelming feeling, more like a voice, that said, "Tell the story of Me." The feeling, and in fact the voice, was not one of my own making, but was one of our Lord. It was overwhelming and filled me with determination and need.

I have found that my creativity grows more positive as I do things that glorify God. I would challenge you to walk your own path, question your maker, and clear your vision enough to see where He wants you to go. I bet it is to glorify His name, spread love, and recognize the *Underlying Grace* that surrounds your own life!

My wife Christine is central to everything that I do. She is my frontline editor and filter to what is good. I own her more than I can ever repay, and I know that she will never ask to settle up. It is cool when you marry your best friend and soul mate!

My children make my moon and planets move around their orbits…they rock.

My guys from Friday morning. You all rock on your own level. Thank you for your trust and letting me go on and on. Pass the pepper!

I would also like to call out Dan, Kathe, and Trip for their reading prowess and comments. You three will always get an advanced copy!

I would like to thank Kathleen Stahl for her spot on editorial abilities and stiff upper lip when it comes to my own version of commas.

Finally, take a look at a movement in Honduras that just might change your heart: www.elhogar.org

Also, GAP Mission is real. We are trying to figure out how to make it so, but it is real. Be a part of it! www.gapmission.com

Look for the next book; *Mighty to Save*. Josh, Neil's son, has to struggle with his own faith, the results of child slavery, and how to survive a plane crash in the jungles of Central America.

You can always stay in touch with me and what is happening with the next books at www.GAllenMercer.com or www.facebook.com/GAllenMercer or www.twitter.com/GAllenMercer

Finally, I would like to thank God. You are the whispering voice that booms. You are the Old Man on my path. I love you, too.

Made in the USA
San Bernardino, CA
18 February 2014